*"Monique, I would like you to come and work for me. In Italy. As Benito's nanny."*

She stared. "You know nothing about me."

"I know that my son loves and trusts you. I suspect Anita did as well if she allowed you to babysit her child. That's a good enough reference for me."

When she said nothing, he gestured toward Benny fast asleep in her lap. "I just saw how good and kind you were to him. You love my son, I think."

Tears filled her eyes. She ducked her head, but suspected he'd seen them anyway. He had the kind of eyes that rarely missed anything. He named a salary that made her sag. Dear God. With that kind of money, she could...

"What do you say, Monique Thomas?"

She pulled in a breath, blinking hard, and then lifted her head. He had an arrogant confidence that should've irked her, but she found it strangely comforting—he wanted what was best for his son. He wanted his son to be happy. That made him powerfully attractive.

She laughed at herself. A man showed a modicum of interest in a child's welfare and she turned to mush? *Really, Monique?*

Dear Reader,

I've always loved a good Cinderella story. There's something wonderfully satisfying about seeing a woman who's good and kind and decent whisked into a glamorous, sophisticated world of wealth and privilege. Especially when she's down on her luck and doesn't have two dimes to rub together.

The Cinderella of this story, Monique, is exactly the kind of woman who deserves a fresh start. While she might be a graduate of the school of hard knocks, she's lost neither her kindness nor her sense of humor. Luca, while not a literal prince, has all the princely virtues—he's strong, sexy and honorable—but he's weighed down with too many worries. If he doesn't want to lose his one chance at happiness, he better hurry because the clock's ticking. It'll be midnight before he knows it. And we all know what happens at midnight.

We all deserve to indulge in a little fairy-tale fantasy from time to time, don't you think? I hope Monique and Luca's story sweeps you away from the real world for a few happy hours and leaves you sighing in satisfaction as you close the final pages.

Hugs and happy reading!

*Michelle*

# Cinderella and the Brooding Billionaire

*Michelle Douglas*

HARLEQUIN®

*Romance*™

Recycling programs
for this product may
not exist in your area.

ISBN-13: 978-1-335-40682-8

Cinderella and the Brooding Billionaire

Copyright © 2021 by Michelle Douglas

This edition published by arrangement with Harlequin Books S.A.

For questions and comments about the quality of this book, please contact us at CustomerService@Harlequin.com.

Harlequin Enterprises ULC
22 Adelaide St. West, 40th Floor
Toronto, Ontario M5H 4E3, Canada
www.Harlequin.com

Printed in U.S.A.

**Michelle Douglas** has been writing for Harlequin since 2007 and believes she has the best job in the world. She lives in a leafy suburb of Newcastle, on Australia's east coast, with her own romantic hero, a house full of dust and books, and an eclectic collection of '60s and '70s vinyl. She loves to hear from readers and can be contacted via her website, michelle-douglas.com.

## Books by Michelle Douglas

### Harlequin Romance

*A Baby in His In-Tray*
*The Million Pound Marriage Deal*
*Miss Prim's Greek Island Fling*
*The Maid, the Millionaire and the Baby*
*Redemption of the Maverick Millionaire*
*Singapore Fling with the Millionaire*
*Secret Billionaire on Her Doorstep*
*Billionaire's Road Trip to Forever*

Visit the Author Profile page
at Harlequin.com for more titles.

To Mr. Ian Malcolm and Mrs. Janina Sulikowski, two wonderful teachers who fostered and encouraged my love and appreciation for stories and storytelling. I am forever in your debt.

## Praise for
## Michelle Douglas

"Michelle Douglas writes the most beautiful stories, with heroes and heroines who are real and so easy to get to know and love.... This is a moving and wonderful story that left me feeling fabulous.... I do highly recommend this one. Ms. Douglas has never disappointed me with her stories."

—*Goodreads* on *Redemption of the Maverick Millionaire*

# CHAPTER ONE

THE BABY WOULD not stop crying.

Luca Vieri paced the floor of his motel room, dragging a hand through his hair. He'd made sure the baby wasn't hungry, that his nappy was dry, that he wasn't running a temperature. And yet the boy continued to cry.

Luca completed a full circuit of the room, which, given the room's size and the length of his legs, took no time at all. The room lacked both the size and luxury he was used to. Though he suspected the spectacular view of the beach from the open front door more than made up for it in most guests' eyes. He cared for neither the lack of luxury nor the view. All he wanted was to be able to comfort his son.

'Luca, are you still there?'

The voice at the other end of the line recalled him to the task at hand. Covering his other ear with his hand, he did what he could to focus on the report his assistant had just given him. *'Sì.'*

The baby continued to cry.

His son, it seemed, had a healthy set of lungs. *His son.*

He closed his eyes but forced them open again a moment later. Once his phone call was finished, he could again give his full attention to the baby.

Perhaps he could step inside his bedroom, close the door, and finish his phone call in semi-quiet, before reapplying himself to the task of soothing his son.

But he didn't have the heart to abandon seven-month-old Benito for even the few minutes that would take. He wanted his son to trust him, to realise he was going to be there for him, that just because things might be hard at the moment he had no intention of letting them scare him off.

'There is no issue with any of that,' he said, striding back into the main part of the motel room, his heart plunging to his feet at Benito's red-faced misery. Soon that misery would give way to hiccups and exhausted sleep.

Luca's hand clenched so hard around his phone it started to ache. With a force of will he loosened his grip. 'Reschedule it all to next week.'

'Already done.'

'Good.' He approached the child's cage—*playpen*—but when Benito's cries grew louder, he backed off, his heart burning. He so badly wanted to comfort his son, but they'd known each other for two days. The child didn't know him, didn't trust him...was still a little frightened of him.

Benito only let him feed him when he became desperately hungry and only fell asleep in his arms when he was desperately exhausted. But he'd woken from a nap earlier, had allowed Luca to give him his lunch…yet now whenever Luca tried to give him the bottle of cool boiled water, he batted it away. Whenever he tried to give him the dummy, he turned his head away. Whenever he picked him up, he struggled to be free.

He wanted to find a quick fix for his son's distress, but there was no quick fix for grief. Benito missed his mother.

This wailing, it was grief for the woman Benito would now grow up without and would never remember. Luca's throat thickened. He wanted to wail against the fates too.

'Luca?'

His assistant's voice snapped him back. 'Sorry, Piero. As for my mother…tell her I will speak to her when I return to Rome.'

'Yes, sir.'

Luca made a note to give his assistant a substantial Christmas bonus at the end of the year. 'I know it is asking a lot. I will also text her the same message, but I fear she will continue to hound you.'

'No matter. I can deal with Signora Conti.'

Very few people could, but Piero was one of them. '*Grazie*, Piero.'

'You need time with your son.'

His lips twisted. 'Except a business empire like The Vieri Corporation refuses to wait patiently while I do that.' He'd only been CEO for two years. Today, though, it felt like twenty.

'Your cousin, Signorina Rosetta Vieri, has stepped in to pick up what slack she can. She is doing an admirable job.'

Luca's gut clenched. Rosetta was the only one of his cousins he fully trusted. They'd recently discovered that the corporation had a traitor in its midst, and he hated leaving her to deal with it on her own. 'Have there been further financial irregularities?'

'*Sì*. Nothing too significant but troubling all the same.'

Hunting down the source of those irregularities would be his top priority when he returned to Rome.

Benito's continued crying filled Luca's head, making it throb, making it increasingly difficult to focus on anything else. He seized the teddy bear he'd bought as a gift and danced it along the railing of the playpen, but Benito merely flung himself to the other side, almost falling against the wooden bars in his haste to avoid his father.

Luca's throat thickened. He loved his son. From the very first moment he'd clapped eyes on Benito, a fierce protectiveness had taken up residence inside his chest. He would create a strong unbreakable bond with his son, would make sure Benito knew he was loved and cherished.

He dragged a hand down his face. It was unreasonable to expect that to happen immediately. These early days were always going to be difficult.

He just hadn't realised they'd wring him so dry. He was used to solving problems, not feeling so…*helpless*.

'There is something else,' his assistant said. 'Signor Romano has been calling. He demands you speak to him personally as soon as you can.'

*Dio!* How had the other man found out about this so quickly?

The baby's wailing was reaching a crescendo in his head. Keeping one eye on his son, he opened the glass sliding door onto the back balcony of his room, welcomed the fresh bite of the breeze on his face. 'You think I need to call him before I return to Rome?'

'*Si.*'

*Cavolo!* He would need to tread carefully, bring into play all his tact and diplomacy. And even then it might not be enough. 'Leave it with me.'

He'd promised Bella he would find a way to break off their engagement. Discovering he had an unknown son provided them with a plausible enough excuse. Luca could claim he needed time to adapt to this new reality. Bella could claim she did not wish to become a stepmother so soon.

Except Signor Romano would argue that Benito's existence made no difference. He would argue for the children of Bella and Luca's marriage to become the legitimate Vieri heirs, rather than Benito, and if that could be settled Bella would become reconciled to raising Benito.

What the older man didn't know, however, was that Bella was in love with another man.

And Luca had no desire to marry a woman who did not wish to marry him.

And while he sorely wanted the union between their families, he had no intention of treating Benito differently from any other children he might one day have.

Given time, without Luca on the scene, Bella might possibly reconcile her father to her chosen man. Still, Signor Romano had a fiery temper, and a merger between the two families was his dearest wish. Luca had to find a way to keep the older man onside, while reconciling him to the fact that Bella and Luca would not marry.

His shoulders sagged at the Herculean task Bella had set him. He would not be able to settle the issue, appease Signor Romano and restore peace in a single phone call, but he could begin to lay the groundwork.

If only Benito would stop crying. If only Luca had managed some sleep in the last three days. If only he'd known about his son seven months ago!

'Okay, Piero—' he ground back a sigh '—give me your impressions of the situation.'

He forced himself to concentrate on his assistant's voice, but a movement inside the motel room caught his attention. The black skirt, white shirt and sensible shoes informed him it was a member of the housekeeping staff. He hadn't heard her call out to identify herself over Benito's cries.

He went to move into the room and ask her to come back later, but the smile that stretched across her face when she glimpsed his son halted him in his tracks.

She swooped down towards the crying child. 'Hello, Benny boy! What's all this fuss you're making?'

Benito immediately stopped crying to swing around and stare at the maid. And then his little arms lifted to be picked up, his urgency evident in the way he bounced on his bottom.

Luca's heart stuttered in his chest.

She picked him up, two tiny arms went about her neck and she cuddled him close, rocking him as he snuffled into her shoulder and neck. She crooned to his son in a low voice, but Luca caught, 'Poor, poor baby,' and 'You miss her too,' and 'Beautiful Benny boy.'

This woman had known Anita?

He shook himself. Of course she had. This

town was no bigger than a postage stamp. Everyone here would know everyone else.

He stared at the woman and child and an ache rose inside him.

She glanced around at him with clear amber eyes. He blinked and straightened. He hadn't realised she'd known he was there. She gestured towards the sofa and he nodded.

Prising her caramel-coloured hair from Benito's fingers, she started to sing a children's song Luca knew from his own childhood. Benito stared up at her with tear-streaked eyes as if she were the answer to all his prayers, and renewed energy began to trickle into every tired atom of Luca's body.

He longed for his son to look at him like that.

'Aren't you going to sing with me, beautiful boy?' this lovely smiling woman said to the child, and Benito broke into the biggest smile that Luca had ever seen.

His son's smile… *Dio!* It was like sunshine and holidays and the Mediterranean in spring.

'Luca, are you still there?'

'I'm sorry, Piero, I have to go. I will call you back.' He pocketed his phone and stepped back into the room.

The maid sang, Benito made cooing noises as if he were trying to copy her and clapped both of his little hands against her larger one—so happy at that moment it made Luca's heart ache.

Without warning, those amber eyes glanced up into his again. Though heaven only knew what he meant by warning, just…such eyes should come with a warning, surely?

*Sing*, she mouthed.

So he sang along with the song too. The baby jerked to stare at him, but the magician of a maid bounced her charge on her lap to make him laugh again. When the song came to an end, she clapped her hands. 'Yay! High five!'

Benito slapped his hand to hers.

'And yay!' she repeated. 'Daddy knows the song too! High five, Daddy!'

Luca held his hand up immediately and Benito smacked his hand to Luca's palm with something midway between a smile and a frown.

But the maid—this glorious, wonderful woman—didn't give *her Benny boy* a chance to ponder, worry or otherwise regret the presence of the man who'd taken a seat beside them on the sofa. Instead, she tickled him until he was a writhing mass of giggles.

When Benito was contentedly sucking his dummy and growing sleepy in her lap, the woman made as if to rise, but Luca touched her wrist. 'Please, stay, just for a little longer.'

She stared at his hand and he immediately pulled it back, suddenly aware of how warm and soft her skin felt beneath his fingertips, like silk and sun. The tips of his fingers throbbed, and he

curled them into his palm. She smelled like va-
nilla and lemon, and perturbingly enticing.

He shot to his feet and moved away. 'You knew
Anita?' It wasn't really a question.

'We were good friends. She worked here at the
motel as well.'

Anita had been a maid? If he'd known she'd
borne his son he'd have made sure she'd lived
like a princess.

'I've babysat Benny many a time.' She smiled
down at the slumbering child. 'We're the best of
friends, Benny and me.'

'*Sì*, I can see that.'

She glanced back up at him quickly and he
shrugged. 'He will allow me to give him his bottle. He will suffer me to change his nappy. He will
only fall asleep in my arms when he is completely
exhausted and can fight sleep no more. He does
not smile at me.'

'Mr Vieri, it will take time.'

She knew his name? Of course she knew his
name. Everyone in Mirror Glass Bay probably
knew his name.

She glanced around the motel room. 'This is
all so new and unfamiliar to him. And he misses
his mother.'

He should have stayed at Anita's cottage,
rather than dragging Benito to the motel. It was
just... He'd felt as if he'd been invading Anita's
privacy. His own discomfort, though, shouldn't

have mattered. What mattered was what was best for Benito.

And what was best for Benito was this magician of a maid.

He studied her left hand, noticed she bore no sign of a wedding ring. In fact, she wore no adornment at all other than a pair of silver studs in her ears. 'You have me at a disadvantage,' he said. 'You know my name, but I do not know yours.'

That generous mouth widened into a smile, and she held out her hand. 'Monique Thomas. It's nice to meet you, Mr Vieri.'

He liked her easy frankness, the innate egalitarian attitude that seemed so much a part of the Australian culture. She must know he was one of the richest men in all of Italy and yet she treated him as she would any other person. He liked that.

He shook her hand. 'Please, call me Luca. And the pleasure is all mine.'

The faintest pink tinged her cheeks. She pulled her hand from his and glanced back at Benito. 'I really should get to work.'

'I have a proposition for you, Monique.'

She swung back, her eyebrows disappearing beneath her fringe.

'A business proposition,' he assured her. Though it suddenly occurred to him that such a lovely-looking woman must get other kinds of propositions all the time.

Sexual interest momentarily flared, but he

ruthlessly extinguished it. Not the time and certainly not the place. To all intents and purposes, the world thought him engaged to be married. While it wasn't true, he couldn't afford to create speculation or scandal.

Monique tried to quell the ridiculous racing of her heart. Anita had told her Benito's father was handsome, but Luca Vieri wasn't just handsome, he was dynamic, devastating…and drop-dead gorgeous.

She swallowed. 'A business proposition?'

Of course he'd meant a *business* proposition. She wasn't the kind of woman who received indecent propositions from rich, powerful, gorgeous men. And even if she were, she wasn't the kind of woman to accept them.

*Little Miss Perfect. Miss Manners. Stuck up and buttoned up.*

She ignored the childhood taunts to focus on the man in front of her. He'd moved to stare out of the glass door at the motel's pool and gardens, his shoulders tight. The discovery that he had a son looked to have turned his world upside down.

Either that or he was a very good actor.

The jury was still out on that.

A business proposition? She'd bet he was going to ask her to babysit Benny for the duration of his stay in Mirror Glass Bay. She calculated the number of occupied rooms in the motel at the moment and nodded. That could be arranged. Eve and Cassidy would do all they could to accommodate him.

And it'd give her a bit more time to say goodbye to Benny. Obviously Luca hadn't made the connection yet that she was his son's godmother.

He swung from the window, those dark intense eyes fixing on her again. They made her swallow…and for some reason feel guilty. She had no reason to feel guilty. If anyone should feel guilty it should be him!

She frowned. Except she wasn't sure about that either and she wasn't jumping to conclusions.

'Monique, I would like you to come and work for me. In Italy. As Benito's nanny.'

She stared. She shook herself. 'You know nothing about me.'

'I know that my son loves and trusts you. I suspect Anita did as well if she allowed you to babysit her child. That's a good enough reference for me.'

When she said nothing, he gestured towards Benny fast asleep in her lap. 'I just saw how good and kind you were to him. You love my son, I think.'

Tears filled her eyes. She ducked her head, but suspected he'd seen them anyway. He had the kind of eyes that rarely missed a thing. He named a salary that made her sag. Dear God. With that kind of money she could…

'What do you say, Monique Thomas?'

She pulled in a breath, blinking hard, and then lifted her head. 'Are you aware that I'm Benny's godmother?'

He fell into the sofa opposite as if her words had knocked the breath from his body. 'God-mother?'

She nodded.

'But…' his face lit up '…this is perfect!'

He had an arrogant confidence that should've irked her, but she found it strangely comforting— he wanted what was best for his son, he wanted his son to be happy. That made him powerfully attractive.

She laughed at herself. A man showed a modi-cum of interest in a child's welfare and she turned to mush?

*Really, Monique!*

'I'd love to be Benny's nanny and it'd be be-yond exciting to visit Italy—' she started to reply.

'Then this is perfect! Let us shake hands on it. I will square everything with your employers, and we can leave as soon as the arrangements can be made. Benito has a passport so we can be quick.'

He rose, tapping a finger against perfectly sculpted lips, his mind racing behind dark eyes that hadn't noticed the sagging of her shoulders or seen the way she'd started to shake her head.

'How long will it take for you to be ready to

leave? You will have my entire apparatus at your disposal.'

'I'm sorry, Luca, but as much as I would love to accept your proposition, I can't.' She swallowed down the lump in her throat. 'I'm sorry.'

He sat again, staring at her with those throbbing eyes. It was like being in the eye of a storm—all eerie quiet before the wind picked you up and flung you every which way.

'You say you love my son; you tell me you would like to travel, and I know that financially my offer is an attractive one.'

'Correct on each count.'

'Are you married or in a relationship?'

'It's nothing like that.' At least, not in the way he meant.

He pursed his lips. 'You have a child?'

She hesitated. Not exactly. At least, not yet.

'Your child would be most welcome. He or she would be a playmate for Benito.'

That was a lovely sentiment. However… 'I'm afraid it's not that simple.'

He leaned towards her. 'Can you not tell me why?'

If she weren't Benny's godmother, nothing would compel her to expose her family's dirty linen to a complete stranger. But Benny was her godson and she owed it to both him and Anita to maintain as much contact with him as possible. She might not be able to accompany Benny to

Italy, but perhaps Luca could be prevailed upon to let her have video calls with the little boy… and maybe real face-to-face visits in the future.

But that wouldn't happen if Luca didn't think her invested in his son's future. And she would hate for Benny to ever think all of his friends in Australia had forgotten about him.

'Monique?'

Dear Lord, when the man said her name in his beautiful Italian accent like that, it could melt a mere mortal to marshmallow. Absurdly, then, she found herself having to blink back tears.

Except it wasn't absurd.

Rising, she took Benny through to the bedroom and placed him in the cot that had been set up in there. She made sure he had his special favourite plush animal nearby—a giraffe with a long neck perfect for little fingers to hold onto. Anita had dubbed the giraffe Colin. She made a mental note to tell Luca about Colin—the comfort and sense of security it gave Benny—and to warn him to always make sure Colin was near…to be careful not to lose him.

She touched a hand to Benny's hair. 'Oh, Anita,' she whispered. 'We miss you.'

When she returned to the main room, Luca held a cup of tea out to her. 'I did not know how you took it.'

'White, no sugar. But black is fine. Thank you.'

She went to take a grateful sip, but her cup was whisked away before she could. 'There is milk.'

It was returned to her a moment later. She sipped, closing her eyes in appreciation. 'Perfect.'

When she opened them again, she found him staring at her with an arrested expression on his face. He shook himself and gestured her to the sofa again.

'Now tell me why you cannot be Benito's nanny, when it is clear that you would like to be very much. And when I would do anything I could to provide my son with the continuity he needs to settle into his new life.'

She smothered a sigh but pasted on a smile. 'If you want continuity then you need to know about Colin.'

He listened intently as she told him about Benny's favourite toy. 'A comfort toy? Yes, I have heard of such things.' That dark head nodded, the expression a little fierce. 'I will buy another—no, I will buy several—and put them in a safe place in case the original ever meets with a mishap.'

That fierceness pressed into the service of his son's happiness gave her pause. It didn't gel that a man like that, someone so protective of his child, would ignore that child's existence for seven months. Which meant someone else in the Vieri family had to have known. And had kept it from him. Who would do such a thing?

Not that she had any intention of posing the question. It was all just conjecture anyway.

'Now, come, tell me what is preventing you from accompanying Benito to Rome?'

At that moment she almost believed he'd slay any dragons that needed slaying—for his son's benefit, of course. Despite the fact it had more to do with Benny than herself, it was still devastatingly attractive. What a shame, then, that the fire-breathing dragon threatening her peace of mind couldn't be conquered so easily.

She set her tea down and forced her shoulders back. 'I recently started proceedings to contest custody of my young niece.'

His gaze darkened. 'Go on.'

'My sister is an addict—drug and alcohol. So is my mother.'

'I see.'

She doubted that. She doubted drug or alcohol addiction had ever touched this man's rarefied world. And she was glad of it. She wished to God they'd not touched hers either.

'I had guardianship of Fern, my niece, while my sister served a custodial sentence for drug dealing. From the moment she was born, though, Fern spent more time living with me than her mother. Skye would occasionally make noises about becoming more hands on, but...'

She trailed off and he nodded, his mouth grim.

'I really thought that she meant to turn her

life around when she was released from prison. I thought she'd learned her lesson. She came to stay with me, and I got her a job here at the motel.'

'You had high hopes?'

She nodded.

'What happened?'

Their mother had happened. She'd blown into Mirror Glass Bay with her insults and her challenges, and with that inexplicable hold that seemed to seduce Skye every single time.

'Did she return to drugs?' Luca asked.

It took all her strength to not drop her head to her hands. 'She stole my credit card and disappeared.' She was still paying off that debt.

'Did you not report her?'

She should have. She could see that now.

He must've read the answer in her eyes. He shook his head. 'Monique...'

Her chest burned. 'My sister was once my world, Luca. When I was a child, my mother couldn't be relied on. But when I was four, she came home from the hospital with Skye. That changed my life, gave me someone to love and something to fight for. Having Skye in my life stopped me from becoming just like my mother.'

He rested his elbows on his knees, the action angling him closer to her. For no reason at all, her heart picked up speed. She took a hasty gulp of her tea. 'She left Fern with me, though, so I figured I'd just keep looking after her and be able to keep her safe.'

'What changed to make you contest custody? You have involved your local authorities, yes?'

She nodded, staring down at her hands. 'Skye and my mother came, with a policeman, and took Fern away.'

His quick intake of breath told her what he thought of that. 'How old is your niece?'

'Three and a half.'

'And how did she react to this?'

The question made her flinch. She shook her head. She refused to put that scene into words. Every time she recalled the way Fern had screamed and cried and clung to her, the hot scald of tears made her throat ache.

She forced her chin up. 'Because I'm not Fern's mother, I have no rights.'

His eyes flashed. 'You have the rights of common decency and to protect those weaker than you.'

She'd not been able to protect Skye from her mother's influence when they'd been growing up. Maybe that was why she was so determined to do all she could to protect Fern now.

'What has happened since this time? How long has it been since this happened?'

'Four months.'

She saw his protest before he could utter it and she held up a hand. 'Please, Luca, I know.'

He snapped his mouth shut.

'I don't believe in taking a child away from their parent except in the direst of circumstances. I hoped rather than believed my sister meant to build a proper relationship with Fern, but the truth of the matter is she and my mother are simply holding Fern to ransom.'

'Explain this to me, please.'

'My sister tells me she will give me custody of Fern in exchange for two hundred thousand dollars.' Her lips twisted. 'I don't have that kind of money. And the bank won't lend it to me.'

'You cannot pay this blackmail because it will not stop! Unless you have legal papers drawn up and—'

She held up her hand again and he halted mid-sentence. 'There's a more pressing concern, Luca. My mother, sister and Fern all live in the same house, and while they're not unkind to Fern they neglect her.'

'You are frightened for her safety?'

*Terrified.*

'I visit as often as I can.' Surprise visits. She never told them when she was coming. 'They live in a larger town forty minutes away. I take groceries so that Fern has something to eat.' And just so she had a chance to hug her little niece and tell her she loved her and was doing everything she could to make sure she could come and live with her for good.

Her heart started to thud. 'Three months ago, when I dropped in unannounced, the house was wide open, but my mother and sister had both passed out in the lounge room and there was food burning on the stove. Fern had been locked in her bedroom.'

Luca's entire body stiffened. He muttered something in Italian. It sounded like an oath. Whatever it was, she found herself nodding. She hated to think what would've happened if she hadn't shown up. They could've burned the house down, with everyone inside it. 'That's when I called Social Services. They've been investigating ever since.'

'But that was three months ago!'

'My mother knows how to play the system. And it's a big thing to take a child from its mother.'

'But—'

'I know. And I've given up hoping that Skye will become a proper mother. I've had to harden my heart against my sister for Fern's sake. Fern deserves to be safe and she deserves to be loved.'

She knew this man agreed with her. She hesitated, but then stood and pulled her right arm from her cardigan. She angled her body so he could see her arm, could see the scar that ran down its length. 'I don't want this happening to my niece.'

# CHAPTER TWO

LUCA STARED AT the burn scar that seemed to go from where Monique's arm met her shoulder to halfway down her forearm and everything inside him started to shake with a rage he'd never before experienced. 'How——?'

He broke off to try and control the fury in his voice. This woman deserved admiration, consideration, not anger and outrage.

'How old were you?' he tried again in a lower voice.

'Nearly five.'

Just a little older than her niece. 'What happened?'

She shrugged her arm back into her cardigan. 'My mother had put chips into a saucepan of hot fat to cook for our dinner. Our oven was broken,' she added as if she saw the question in his eyes. 'She'd set the timer and when it went off, I tried to find her, but she was nowhere in the house.'

'So you tried to take the saucepan off the stove?'

'It was heavier than I thought it'd be.'

She didn't go on and he didn't have the heart to ask additional questions that could only cause her pain. Her mother should be flayed alive for her neglect.

'So you can see that, as much as I would love to come to Italy as Benny's nanny, I can't abandon my niece.'

'Of course you cannot. Your Fern needs you.' And he suspected she needed her Fern.

He was going to fix this. And he didn't care how much it cost him. What was the point in being wealthy if he couldn't do good things with his money?

Monique tossed her head and caramel curls danced about her shoulders. 'Now that you know about my family, I...'

'You...?'

She pressed her hands together. She hadn't taken her seat again after rising to show him her arm, and he couldn't help thinking that she was like a bird poised for flight if he made the slightest wrong move. He made a silent vow to do his best to not make a wrong move.

'I should imagine I'm not the kind of woman you'd want in charge of your son.'

He blinked. 'Why not?'

Her eyes widened. Caramel eyes and caramel hair. This woman would taste delicious.

The thought, odd and unsettling, whispered through him. He realised then that the tension wrapping him tightly hid another emotion besides anger at those who should've kept Monique safe. Desire had become a liquid heat in his veins. This woman tempted his every sense in a way no woman had in a very long time. He wanted to feast on her warmth and her smiles, satiate the need that surged through his blood.

He tried to shake it away. She was nothing like the women from his world.

Which could be why he wanted her.

Or maybe the barriers he normally erected around himself had taken a beating when he'd discovered he had a son, and he hadn't had the time to fix them back into place.

He forced himself to straighten. He would not be dallying with this woman, regardless of how lovely she was. He didn't mix business with that kind of pleasure, and he still had high hopes she'd become Benito's nanny.

Neither could he forget that in the world's eyes he was engaged to Bella Romano. Once the news broke of the cancelled engagement, if he did not wish to alienate Bella's father, he would have to wait a decent interval before his name was linked with another woman's.

He'd go to whatever lengths were necessary to prevent such an eventuality. Signor Romano was crucial to Luca's plans for re-establishing the former glory of the Vieri name and reputation. He'd promised his grandfather that he'd restore the family's honour, and he refused to let the older man down. He owed his grandfather everything.

Monique had still not answered his question about why he should now not wish to employ her. He worked hard to keep his voice pleasant. 'Are you dependent on either drugs or alcohol?'

She drew herself up. 'Absolutely not.'

It was as he'd thought. 'You cannot choose your family so why would I judge you based on their actions and attitudes?' He held her gaze. 'Anita trusted you with her son. She made you his godmother. That is a good enough reference for me.'

Something in her face gentled and things inside him yearned towards it, but he cut them off with a ruthlessness born of need. 'I wish to ask you something. Do you know why Anita never told me about Benito?'

She hesitated. 'It was my understanding that she had.'

His temples started to throb. 'Obviously Benito inherits all of Anita's worldly goods. I, as Benito's father, will hold it in trust for him until he comes of age. I have been over the documentation with her lawyer. It appears Anita came into a large sum of money recently.'

She gnawed on her bottom lip, her eyes losing their sparkle. 'I thought that had come from you.'

He stiffened.

'But it appears Benny's existence has come as a surprise to you.' One slim shoulder lifted. 'I'm sorry. All I can tell you is that Anita told me she'd tried to contact you.'

Ice settled beneath his breastbone.

'She never told me your name, but she always spoke of you with a great deal of fondness.' She smiled, as if remembering her friend's actual words, and that those words had all been good. 'She told me it was a holiday fling.'

That's exactly what it had been—an act of rebellion before he buckled down to the path his grandfather had formulated to win back the family's reputation. He'd relinquished the last vestiges of dreams that had somehow survived—dreams of love and freedom.

He hadn't realised he still believed in such things. He'd thought they'd all been destroyed when he was twenty years old, hadn't realised such sentimentality still had a hold on him.

After what had happened with Camilla one would've thought he'd have learned his lesson. But one bad apple didn't mean every other woman in the world was bad as well. Besides, Camilla hadn't been all bad either, just tempted beyond endurance. She'd taken the money and run. A part of him even understood it.

But it had certainly made him wary. How did one tell real love from fake when they looked so alike?

True love? He bit back a snort. One might as well wish for unicorns and a genie! No, an arrangement where both parties knew exactly what they were getting from the marriage was the smarter choice. That way no one could be disappointed.

Monique's low laugh snapped him back. 'Anita told me it was every dream of a holiday fling that one could ever have, making me wildly envious.'

The words should've been a gift. And yet Anita had betrayed him too. Monique's revelation confirmed the suspicion that had been growing in his mind. 'Someone in my family paid Anita to keep her quiet. She took a bribe.'

Monique's chin lifted. 'She accepted child support that she was entitled to,' she corrected. 'That's a very different thing.'

She'd accepted money in exchange for her silence. She'd kept his son from him!

'Who would offer her such a bribe?' she said.

'My parents. If I'd known she was pregnant, I'd have married her. They'd have known that.'

Her eyes flashed. 'You're very confident. Please, don't be offended if I correct you and say you'd have *offered* to marry her.'

*Touché.* Perhaps he'd become too used to women throwing themselves at him.

*Not you, but your family's money.*

'And why would your parents do something so…?'

Heinous? Spiteful? Abhorrent? He shook his head. 'They have previous form.'

Though she didn't move, he sensed her drawing away from him. 'You have other children that they've kept from you?'

'No!' He dragged a hand down his face. 'I mean that in the past my father once paid a woman a substantial amount of money to break up with me. Apparently, he and my mother had deemed her unsuitable.'

The smooth perfection of her brow pleated. 'That's...*awful.*' She swallowed, her hands pressed against her stomach. 'I'm really sorry, Luca.'

He had a feeling she meant every word.

'But you're wrong if you think that's what Anita did. She had integrity, but she also had her pride. She'd accept child support for Benny's sake, but she wouldn't beg you to be a part of his life if she didn't think that's what you wanted.'

'She should've known I—'

'I don't think a six-day fling on a tropical island, even given all you shared, qualifies either of you to claim to know the other well.'

He dragged in a breath. That was true enough.

'Please, don't harbour a sense of injury towards her.'

He could see the thought of it broke her heart. It made things inside him tighten and loosen, both at the same time.

'Please, just accept the fact she was a good

person and would never have kept Benny from you knowingly.'

It occurred to him then that with very little evidence to the contrary Monique had believed the best of him. After seeing him with Benito, seeing for herself how much his son's happiness meant to him, she'd made the decision to accept what he said at face value. She was right. It would be pointless to hold a grudge towards Anita. 'All you say is true. Very well, I will simply regard it as…an unfortunate series of circumstances that led to a misunderstanding.'

Her eyes narrowed. 'Due to the interference of third parties.'

He also knew it would be pointless to confront his parents. They'd only deny it. All he could do was cherish Benito from this day forward. 'It will be best,' he agreed, 'to turn my face to the future.'

Excellent plan.' She nodded her approval and then lifted a hand. 'I'm sorry, but I really need to get to work now.'

'If I clear it with your employer, will you be Benito's nanny for the duration of my stay?' He had to work hard to keep his voice even.

'Yes, gladly.' She hesitated. 'At some stage I'm hoping to talk to you about ways I can remain in contact with Benny once you leave.'

'We will work something out,' he promised. 'I will go and speak to Eve and Cassidy immediately.'

Her smile could slay a man where he stood. He left before he did something reckless like press a kiss to the golden skin of her cheek and drag a deep breath of her into his lungs like some hormone-riddled teenager.

He spoke to Eve and Cassidy and Eve's husband Damon about more than hiring Monique in the short term. He told them he wanted to hire Monique as Benito's full-time nanny for the next twelve months. 'She is his godmother, practically family. She loves him and he loves her. It is clear Anita trusted her.'

Eve nodded. 'They were close. We all miss Anita. And we'll miss Monique too if she accepts the position you're offering.'

The two women exchanged glances. One he could interpret with ease. 'Yes,' he agreed, 'there is the matter of her niece.'

Both women blinked.

'She has told me of the situation.'

'She won't leave without her,' Cassidy said from her spot behind the bar. 'She's a mama bear where Fern is concerned.'

Better and better. The more he learned of Monique the surer he became that she was the right person to take charge of his son. 'I mean to do something about that situation.

'Good.' Eve's lips thinned. 'That child should've been placed in Monique's care from the moment she was born.'

Damon straightened from where he slouched against the bar. 'Is there anything we can do to help?'

Luca considered the offer. Damon was a successful businessman with local connections. 'Is there a local lawyer you would recommend—someone smart, hard-nosed and who can think on their feet?'

'I know just the person. What's your phone number? I'll forward the details through to you.'

Luca understood the subtext but gave his number without hesitation. If Monique did come to Rome with him, these people wanted personal access to him, to make sure Monique was treated right. This community looked after their own, and he suspected they considered Benito one of their own too. He liked them all the more for it.

He made the decision then and there to buy Anita's little house. He and Benito would come back here. Often. Or, at least, as often as he could manage. He would provide his son with all the links to his mother that he could.

'If there's anything else we can do…'

'There is strength in numbers,' Luca agreed, 'but in this instance I mean to go in hard and fast and get this done as quickly as possible.'

'Excellent.'

That was Cassidy. She was a very beautiful woman, but there was a dangerous edge to her smile that he didn't understand. 'At some point

Monique and I will need to beard the lion in his den. I would not wish to take Benito into that situation.'

'We'd love to look after Benny,' Eve and Cassidy both said at the same time.

'Thank you.'

He turned to leave but found Cassidy at his elbow. 'Let me see you out.'

She had something to say to him?

'Mr Vieri, I heartily approve of what you're doing for Fern.'

'But?'

'Monique has the kindest heart of anyone I know. She's been let down by the people she should've been able to rely on.' They halted by his car and that dangerous smile became more dangerous. 'If you hurt her or mistreat her, I will hunt you down, and once I'm through with you, you won't be capable of bearing another child. Do I make myself clear?'

He stared, momentarily lost for words, but an absurd smile built inside him. Monique was much loved here in Mirror Glass Bay. He could not have asked for a better reference. 'Signorina Cassidy, if I hurt or mistreat the lovely Monique, I will let you find me and will hold still while you do your worst.'

'Perfect answer.' Cassidy's smile lost its edge. 'I'm glad we're on the same page. Have a nice day.'

She turned and sauntered away. For the first

time in three days Luca felt the sun on his face, heard the surf rolling up the beach just out of sight, and dragged salt-laden air into his lungs. He had a son, a wonderful son, and for a brief moment everything felt right with the world.

It was amazing how quickly money could grease wheels and make things happen, but it still took the best part of a week to get the necessary paperwork in order. He wanted the contract that would give Monique custody of her niece to be watertight.

While waiting for it to be finalised, he moved himself and Benito back into Anita's house. She hadn't owned it, had been renting, but it was where his son had spent the first seven months of his life, so he bought it. He paid more than the market price, but as far as he was concerned it was worth every penny.

While it might be tiny compared to what he was used to, it was also homely and comfortable. Here he could exist in a bubble away from his usual stresses and responsibilities. He could play on the beach with his son and relax. And threaded through it all was Monique, who smoothed *everything*. Who made everything seem easy. Who brought light and joy to Benito's face.

He'd smiled when he'd discovered Monique lived in the house next door. No wonder the two women had become such fast friends. He couldn't have planned that more perfectly if he'd tried.

He didn't tell Monique what he had organised until the morning they set off for her mother's house. She raised her head from the contract he'd handed her, her eyes dazed. 'You've done…?'

'We are going to remove your niece from her current situation and ensure she is properly looked after.'

'You're offering my sister a ridiculous amount of money…' her eyes scanned the page '…to sign custody over to me?'

He didn't consider half a million dollars a ridiculous amount of money. Not when it would ensure the safety of a child. 'Please, let me do this.'

'I've no intention of stopping you. I want Fern safe too much for that. But I will pay you back.'

He took her hands in his. They were cold and he worked at rubbing warmth back into them. 'If you come to Rome for twelve months as Benito's nanny, I will consider myself amply repaid.'

She nodded, but he could see she was too afraid to hope, afraid that something would go wrong.

If he'd judged her sister correctly, nothing would go wrong. She'd be happy to sell her soul, let alone her only child, for the money he was offering.

'Come, the driver and the lawyer are here.'

He'd ordered the driver to collect the lawyer first. 'The lawyer is going to explain exactly how we're to do this.'

It went exactly as Luca expected. The lawyer did most of the talking and Monique's sister and mother couldn't hide the way their eyes lit up when they discovered the amount of money on offer.

He knew what he was doing was sordid, but the entire situation was sordid. If it would give rise to a good outcome for an innocent child, he was prepared to play whatever ugly games were necessary. Especially now he had a son.

He couldn't bear the thought of Benito being neglected or taken advantage of by anyone. *Dio!* What would've happened if Anita hadn't put his name on Benito's birth certificate? It didn't bear thinking about. What he did know was that Monique would've stood by her godson and given him all the love and care that she could. In return, this was the least that he could do for her.

Monique's mother tried to negotiate for more money but was shut down so quickly by the lawyer that Skye reprimanded her. Skye seized a pen and declared herself ready to sign on the dotted line, as if afraid the offer would be withdrawn.

Monique forestalled her. 'Skye, are you really prepared to do this—sign away all rights to Fern?'

Skye tossed her head, her eyes hard. 'She

was always more yours than mine. Besides, this amount of money will change my life. This is a once in a lifetime opportunity. If you think I'm going to let it pass me by, you're stupider than I thought.'

He had to grit his teeth to stop from telling her exactly what he thought. Monique would never part with her niece, not for any amount of money.

'If you continue on your current course, Skye, this amount of money has the potential to kill you,' Monique said in a low voice that throbbed with pain.

*Dio santo!* He had not considered that.

'Who's this?' Monique's mother jeered, gesturing towards him. He saw it for what it was—a tactic to divert Skye's attention. 'Your fancy man?'

Monique's shoulders snapped back. He stepped forward. 'The contract needs to be witnessed. Which I will do.'

Sharlene Thomas laughed. 'You can act as stuck up as you like, Monique, but you're no better than me or your sister.'

What a piece of work! He'd like to—

'It's not too late, Skye,' Monique said.

But Skye ignored her and signed the document in all the spots the lawyer indicated, and Luca forced himself to remain calm and reserved.

'Looks like you've done all right for yourself.' Skye hitched her chin towards Luca. 'And now I'm going to do all right for myself.'

He sensed rather than saw Monique flinch. He had to fight the urge to put an arm around her shoulders and draw her within the protective shelter of his arms, shield her from the barbs and poison of these people who should love her.

The rest of the paperwork was signed with barely another word exchanged.

'I want to sit in your lap!'

Fern's bottom lip wobbled, and all Monique wanted to do was pull her darling niece into her arms and hold her close. 'But we're in the car, pumpkin, and you know the rules.'

Fern banged her heels against her car seat. Luca had been surprisingly well prepared and had ensured the car had one. She wanted to hug him for his forethought, for the provisions he'd made. She could hardly believe that Fern—her darling Fern—was no longer in danger of the harm neglect could inflict. She couldn't believe Fern was now hers to love and look after and protect *forever*.

*Thank you. Thank you. Thank you.*

'I hate the rules!' Fern shouted.

She could focus on her gratitude later. For the moment she needed to do all she could to quieten her niece's fears. She leaned in close to the little girl. 'I love you, my Fern. And you are now going to live with me for ever and ever.'

Two little hands went either side of Monique's face. 'You promise?'

The mistrust in the child's eyes broke her heart. 'I promise, sweetie.'

A sob wrenched from the depths of Fern's chest, and Monique's vision blurred. Luca instructed the driver to pull over and stop the car beside a small park. Monique turned to him.

'You need ten minutes alone with your niece. This has all happened so quickly. There has been no time for explanations and reassurances or...' his face became strangely vulnerable '...cuddles. Take some time to lay your niece's fears to rest, Monique.'

She already owed him so much. 'I know how badly you wanted to get back to Benny and—'

'We have time.'

This small kindness won over every last part of her that his actions in ensuring Fern was removed from her vulnerable situation hadn't already won.

She sat on the grass with Fern in her lap, her arms tight about the little girl, and told her that they were going to live together until Fern was all grown up, and that even then they could still live together if that's what Fern wanted. She told her of all the fun things they would do together, and how they were soon going on a big plane to a place called Italy where they were going to live for a year.

Because, of course, she was accepting the position of Benny's nanny. Given all Luca had done for her, she suspected she'd do just about anything he asked of her now.

She didn't know how much Fern understood, but the tension slowly drained from the little body and she relaxed into Monique. Monique dragged in a couple of deep breaths and revelled in the feeling, the sense of well-being…the relief that Fern was now safe.

Fern sat up to stare at her aunt. 'And Mummy?'

She'd been prepared for the question. 'Mummy can come visit us at any time, but she's not allowed to take you home with her. It's the rules.'

Fern had cried then, and Monique had simply held her.

It wasn't until later, once both children had been put down for naps, that Monique and Luca had a chance to speak. She resisted the urge to throw her arms around his neck and plant a grateful kiss to his cheek. The way he held himself slightly aloof told her that one didn't take such liberties with Luca Vieri. 'I don't know how to thank you.'

'It is not necessary. Is Fern…? I don't know how to say it. At ease, unworried, no longer afraid?'

She nodded. 'This might sound strange, but her show of temper in the car heartened me. She's never been particularly rambunctious, but when she was forced to return to her mother, she became very withdrawn. Even with me. I lost her trust.'

'I am sorry.'

'Don't be. I'll win it back.' She glanced up and then grimaced. 'I'd also like to apologise for the offensive conclusions my mother drew about you.'

'That was not your fault. Besides, what do I care what your mother thinks of me? I urge you to forget it. I have.'

Beneath her ribcage, her heart thudded. 'Luca, I can't thank you enough. I—'

'There is no need.'

He held up a hand, but she ignored it. 'There's every need.'

The coffee had finished brewing and she poured them both a cup, slid one across to him. He shouldn't look at home in Anita's kitchen, but he did. She gestured towards the back door. 'Let's enjoy the sun while we have the chance.'

She led him out to the café table and chairs that sat beneath the shade of a battered-looking frangipani tree. Honeyeaters chirped in a cabbage palm at the bottom of the garden gathering fibres for their nests. In the distance, beneath everything, was the soothing sound of the ocean.

She pulled in a deep breath and released it, feeling a new freedom in both her body and her mind. 'You've made sure my niece is safe. You've changed her life for the better. It's a huge thing that you've done.'

He hesitated, his cup halfway to his mouth. A strangely vulnerable expression stretched through his eyes before the shutters came down over them. 'I had the means to help. We, all of us, should fight injustice when we see it.'

And since he'd discovered he had a son, she suspected it had given him a different perspective on such matters.

'I wasn't only glad to help, I felt privileged to be in a position to help.'

Those dark eyes with their earnest expression could undo a woman.

'So come. Let's hear no more about it.'

Only he would say such a thing.

She tried to not notice the way his lips touched his mug, tried to ignore the warmth it sparked at her very centre, tried not to imagine that mouth doing…other things. Against her better judgement, almost against her will, things inside her softened. Yet some sixth sense warned her against the softening. She was so grateful to this man, but…

They were from different worlds and she couldn't fool herself—the only place he saw for her in his world was as Benny's nanny. Her sole goal now was to make his life as easy as she could. It was the least she could do, given everything he'd done for her and Fern. Getting a crush on him wouldn't make anybody's life easier.

'You've given me my heart's desire.'

His eyes speared back to hers. For the briefest moment she imagined that heat smouldered in their depths. But then he blinked, and it was gone, replaced with his usual calm detachment.

Her heart thundered in her ears. She had to have imagined it. Dear God, if he wanted her…

*No.* She had to nip all such fanciful imaginings in the bud right now.

Seizing her coffee, she took a gulp that burned her throat. Boss and nanny, that was the only relationship they were going to have. Anything further would complicate things. Besides, she'd sworn to never get involved with another emotionally unavailable man again.

And instinct told her Luca was as emotionally unavailable as they came.

She set her mug back down. 'Of course—' her voice was too husky but there was nothing she could do about it '—there's now no question of whether I'll come to Italy or not. I'd be honoured to be Benny's nanny for the next twelve months. I'll be his nanny for as long as you want.'

Competing impulses seemed to war with each other in the depths of his eyes, and she found herself holding her breath. He blinked and her heart sank when she saw that it was detachment that had won. Kindness was there too, but also determination.

'Two things,' he murmured.

She nodded, not taking her eyes from his as she sipped her coffee.

'The first thing you need to know is that what I did for Fern was not conditional on your acceptance of the nanny position. That was a thing apart. To put conditions on it would cheapen it.'

The man was honourable. While the Vieri family were rich, the name didn't come without controversy. But Luca Vieri was an undeniably honourable man. 'Thank you,' she managed. 'I appreciate that. And the second thing?'

'I ask only for twelve months, Monique. I want my son to have continuity until he becomes accustomed to his new life. But this is your home...' he gestured around '...and you love it.'

She did. With the salary Luca had promised her, she could buy a house here and set up her own business. It was a dream come true.

'I want you to understand that for the next twelve months your life will not be your own. The reason I offered such a generous salary is because I want you on call twenty-four seven. I also want you to train two nannies to take over from you when the time comes.'

She hadn't considered the practicalities of the position. He was a new parent, thrust into fatherhood with next to no warning. He might look capable and in control, but she knew how intimidating it could be to have sole responsibility for a child. He was asking a lot of her. She glanced at the house where her niece slept. He'd also given her so much.

'Once we're settled in and you've started to train your replacements, you will have free time. But if for some reason Benito should need you, I want to be able to call you and have you return immediately.'

Well, that wasn't so bad. It meant that eventually she and Fern could do a few hours of sightseeing in the city, along with some shopping.

'Will that be a problem for you?'

'Absolutely not.' Even if it had been she wouldn't have said so. 'Benny is my godson. I love him. It'll be no hardship looking after him.'

'This is also why I want only twelve months of your life.'

It took a moment for her to understand what he meant. When she did her mouth dried. Luca was Benny's father—Benny was Luca's, no one else's. 'Are you going to ask me to give up contact with Benny at the end of all this?'

'No!'

He couldn't have looked more shocked and it eased the burn in her chest.

'I mean to bring Benito back here...' he gestured at the house '...for a holiday every year. I hope you and Fern will still be here, and in addition I hope you will video call with Benito regularly. You are his godmother, Monique. You are a link to his mother. I want him to grow up knowing you.'

She sagged back against the unforgiving wrought iron of her chair. 'That's okay, then.'

'*Si?*'

'It'll be a wrench to leave him at the end of twelve months, of course. There'll be tears on both sides when it's time for me to return home, and you need to be prepared for that. But...' A furrow pressed itself into her brow.

'But?'

'I'm not going to guard my heart in expectation of that eventuality. I mean to love him as much as I can. He's the dearest little boy who deserves all the love in the world.' It's what Anita would've wanted. 'So if that's going to be a problem for you—'

He reached across to clasp her hand and her tongue cleaved to the roof of her mouth. He murmured something in Italian that she didn't understand but which sounded unaccountably beautiful. And then he smiled, and it hit her then how rarely this man smiled.

'No, it is not a problem for me. You are a courageous woman, and that is a blessing for my son.' He surveyed her for several heart-stopping moments. 'So we have a deal, *si*?'

She couldn't help answering his smile with one of her own. She placed her hand in the one he held out and shook it. She knew next to no Italian—which was something she'd have to rectify—but one word she did know was yes. She nodded. '*Si.*'

\* \* \*

They set off for Italy in Luca's private jet a week later. It was proving hard to get her head around the fact that the man who now employed her was one of the wealthiest men in Italy. During the last two weeks he'd simply become Benny's father— a man working hard to forge a solid relationship with his infant son.

The jet brought reality crashing back.

And had nerves jangling in her stomach.

Returning from checking on the children, who were sleeping in beds at the back of the plane, she found Luca tapping away on his laptop. She hesitated in front of him. 'You should get some sleep, Monique,' he said without glancing up. 'It will help with the jet-lag.'

She couldn't sleep. 'I have some questions.'

He glanced up immediately, searched her face and gestured for her to take the seat opposite. 'Just give me a moment to finish this.' He tapped away on his keyboard for a full minute, before closing the lid and giving her his full attention. 'Tell me these questions you have.'

It could be heady being the sole focus of Luca's attention. If a girl let it. She had no intention of letting it do any such thing. 'You've seen the world I come from...'

'Yes.'

She moistened her lips. 'Look, Luca, I knew you were wealthy, but until I stepped on your private jet, I didn't realise… I mean, these last couple of weeks you've just been Benny's father to me and—'

'I am Benny's father.'

'But you're also in charge of one of the world's largest financial dynasties. You have a name to rival Onassis.'

'This is a problem for you?'

That's not what she'd meant. 'It's a change in mindset. I've just realised that I'm not going to be able to take Benny and Fern to play in the local park, am I?'

Understanding dawned in his eyes.

'Given your fortune, Benny would command a huge ransom if he were kidnapped. And even if he isn't at risk of such a thing, the paparazzi will be clamouring for photos of your *"unknown son".*' She made quote marks in the air.

He nodded heavily.

'My naiveté is appalling. You must be regretting hiring me, but I assure you—'

'No.' He pointed a finger at her. 'This I do not regret. This I blame myself for. I did not think to warn you, to make explicit the expectations of your role.'

It's no one's fault,' she replied. 'I just need to know all the things I must do to keep Benny safe, and not create complications for you.'

He nodded slowly. 'Very well, yes. You cannot leave the house unattended. You must always take a driver and a bodyguard with you when you do.'

Wow. Okay.

'Benito is not to leave the villa without my express permission.'

Lord, it was going to be like house arrest. Her ears had picked up one rather lovely word, though. 'You live in a villa, not an apartment? Does that mean you have a garden…maybe a patch of lawn where the children and I can play?'

For some reason her question made his lips twitch. 'Yes, there is room for the children to play.'

That was something at least. Though she wondered if their ideas of 'room to play' were the same thing.

'Any other questions?'

'Just one more.' She frowned again. 'Should I be calling you Signor Vieri rather than Luca?'

# CHAPTER THREE

HE SHOULD NOD. He should tell her to call him Signor Vieri. He should put into place boundaries that could not be crossed, because his every instinct warned him that with this woman he needed all the boundaries that could be enforced.

But he'd grown addicted to the way she saw him, had grown addicted to her softly spoken *Luca*. Found his ears constantly attuned for it.

In her eyes he wasn't the head of one of the wealthiest families in Italy. In her eyes he was a hero, who had won for her her heart's desire. His shoulders went back.

He had little doubt that when Fern's custody case had finally made it to court, the authorities would've placed her in Monique's care. The only problem was how long it would've taken. As far as he was concerned, even one day was too long to wait.

He'd done nothing heroic. He'd splashed around some money, which had solved the problem.

Money he could well afford. Yet no one had ever looked at him the way Monique had.

To tell her she could no longer call him Luca...

'Of course you should continue to call me Luca.'

Her smile and the sweet caramel warmth of her eyes was his reward. She opened her mouth... hesitated.

'There is something else on your mind?'

'I've always been...if not friends at least on friendly terms with most of my previous employers.'

She seemed to choose her words carefully. It made his every sense stand to attention.

Her lips pursed, first to the right and then to the left. 'I fear what I'm about to say will seem unforgivably personal to you and you'll think me impertinent.' She winced. 'And I've no desire to vex you.'

He forced himself to not lean forward. He sensed she needed space, a sense of safety, to ask her question and he didn't wish to crowd her. 'Please, ask your question.'

'A little while ago, as in an hour ago, I did what any normal person would've done when you first offered them a job—I did an internet search on you.'

So that was what had kept her glued to her phone.

She smiled and rolled her eyes. 'Though, of

course, my life has been anything but normal these last couple of weeks.'

Not normal, no. He'd given her her heart's desire. It had created gratitude, but also chaos. He suspected she did not mind the chaos, but her life—all their lives—had changed so quickly. What had she discovered that perturbed her so?

'You are engaged?'

*Ah.*

'Onassis, Vieri... Romano... These names are all so far outside of my reality I feel as Alice must've when she fell down the rabbit hole.' She looked dazed, just as the fictional Alice must have, but still sent him a smile that speared straight into his chest. 'I wish you every happiness, by the way.'

Dear God, this woman and her warmth!

Cassidy's words floated back to him. *'Monique has the kindest heart of anyone I know.'*

Things inside him pulled tight. 'What is your question?'

'What does your fiancée think about this situation?'

Situation? There was no situation! He and Monique were employer and employee. Well, okay, perhaps Monique was more than that—as Benito's godmother she was practically family. And, while he might've won for her her heart's desire, it didn't mean—

'I need to know if she resents Benny or...' Her

brow pleated. 'Or if she's ambivalent about this turn of events. I'm not saying that's not an understandable reaction. It's just… I'd rather be forewarned.'

He closed his eyes. She meant the situation with his son. Of course that was what she meant.

'In accepting the position of Benny's nanny, I made a commitment to look after him to the best of my ability.'

She was asking if she needed to protect Benito from his future stepmother. 'Bella would never hurt a child, would never be unkind to one.'

She let out a breath he hadn't realised she'd been holding, her body relaxing back into her seat. He made a decision then to confide in her. She felt she owed him and while he had no intention of taking advantage of that, it did mean he could trust her.

'Thank you for taking the time to address my concerns.' She started to rise. 'I'll let you get back to your work.'

'Please, sit.'

She blinked and sat.

'What I am about to tell you is confidential.'

She made a zipping motion across her mouth that made him smile.

And focus far too closely on the dusky fullness of her lips. 'It will be best if you know what to expect when we reach Rome.'

He told himself it would be in Benito's best interests if she were furnished with all the relevant information.

'It is not widely known yet, but the engagement between Bella and myself has been cancelled.'

Her hand flew to her mouth. 'Because of Benny?'

He shook his head. He could not let her think that. 'The arrangement was not a love match. That is not how things are done in my world. Both families wanted the match for...business reasons.'

Her jaw dropped. She snapped it back into place, swallowed and nodded. 'I see.'

She didn't see. The entire concept was foreign to her. He could see that in the thinning of her lips and the way the skin around her eyes pulled tight. He didn't want to see this situation through her eyes. She had no notion of the pressures and responsibilities that came with being head of a family like his. She didn't know of the promise he had made to his grandfather. She didn't *need* to know those things.

'Bella, however, has fallen in love with another man. One it's unlikely her father will approve of. Bella confided all of this to me the week before I learned of Benito's existence. She begged me to find some way to break off our engagement.'

'Why doesn't she just break it off herself?'

'She is afraid of her father's disapproval. I have known Bella since we were children. We are friends. I respect her and am fond of her.' The marriage would've been dutiful, companionable. *Boring.*

He did what he could to banish that thought. 'I am happy to help her however I can.'

Monique shifted on her seat. 'So *you* have to take the heat for *her* decision?'

It took all his strength not to drop his head back to the headrest and close his eyes. If he was careful, he could preserve the relationship between himself and Signor Romano. And he would be careful. Very, *very* careful.

Her mouth worked. '*This* is the kind of marriage you plan to make?'

Her incredulity shouldn't sting. His world was alien to her. 'In recent times the Vieri name, as you no doubt know, has been tarnished with scandal and disgrace due to the intemperance of my parents' generation. They—my parents, aunts and uncles—took and took without thought for others, often not paying their bills. They sent merchants and tradespeople out of business with their carelessness, broke up marriages and took advantage of everything and everyone. The Vieri name, which was once synonymous with integrity and prestige, is now—'

He broke off, acid burning his throat. 'They gave nothing back. They cared nothing for the legacy my grandfather and great-grandfather and his father before him worked so hard to build.'

She stared at him. 'But you do. You want to honour their hard work.' Her brow pleated. 'So your marriage to Bella was a step towards winning back that respectability?'

'Yes.'

'And Benny provides you with a convenient excuse to break off the engagement as he's now... your heir?'

'It is not that simple. Things are no longer that archaic.'

'Really? They sound positively medieval to me?' she muttered.

His head rocked back.

She winced. 'I'm sorry, I shouldn't have said that out loud.'

He let it pass. He could imagine how strange she must find this situation. 'Each generation fights it out to decide who will become CEO of the Vieri dynasty.'

'So the fact that Benny is your firstborn doesn't mean anything? Any children you and Bella would've had would have just as much a chance as being the head of the family?'

'Along with their cousins, yes.'

Behind those lovely eyes, her mind raced.

'I can see you have many thoughts on the subject. Will you not share them?'

'It isn't my place.'

'Please?'

He wasn't sure why he insisted, except she'd

have an entirely different perspective on this situation, and he welcomed anything that would give him an advantage in this particular arena.

'Okay,' she started slowly, 'I suspect you have cousins who wish to depose you.'

'Cousins and uncles,' he clarified. Though until recently he'd thought he and his cousins were all on the same page. 'And if they could gain the favour of the board they could do so.'

'I also suspect you have cousins who are glad to let you have the job.'

'That too is true.'

'So if Benny doesn't want to be head of the Vieri family fortune, he won't be forced into it?'

Her concern for his son touched him.

'If he wishes to be an artist or an engineer or head of PR, he could do those things instead?'

'Yes.'

She was quiet for a long moment. 'As CEO, I'm guessing you're in charge of the purse strings. So... Does that mean some members of your family...' she hesitated '...from your parents' generation resent you?'

He didn't answer that directly. 'I have curtailed all unnecessary expenditure.'

Each member of the family received generous remuneration from the stock they held in the company, but it was time certain individuals learned to live within their means instead of constantly skimming the company's profits or dipping into the family reserves. Such unrestrained spending would eventually see the Vieri Corporation in receivership. None of them needed another private jet, luxury yacht or yet another holiday villa.

'They were all in favour of your marriage to Bella?'

'Yes.' Because they thought it would bring more money into the coffers and would, therefore have him loosening the purse strings—an entirely erroneous assumption he hadn't bothered to correct.

'For the next few months I need to be very careful. The Vieri and Romano families do a great deal of business together and it would hurt us both if a rift were to occur.'

'You mean if Bella's father were to take offence that you've called off the engagement with his daughter.'

'He's a powerful man.'

'So are you.'

He stared. But her confidence in him made his shoulders go back. 'Signor Romano's and my values align.'

'The broken engagement doesn't mean you can't still work together, though, surely?'

He'd had such hopes… Maybe she was right. Maybe all hope wasn't lost. 'I have spoken to him several times in the last two weeks. He is angry and disappointed.' He'd almost sounded hurt.

He shook the thought off. He was merely pro-

jecting. It was his own disappointment speaking. Signor Romano was everything he wished his own father could be. 'Signor Romano has not yet reconciled himself to the broken engagement, so...'

'So?'

'I need to be very careful during the next few months to not offend him...to make sure my name is not linked with another woman's.'

Her face cleared. 'Oh, I see.'

He grimaced. 'And yet I will now be considered fair game, so to speak. Therefore, I must also be careful not to give insult to the daughters of other respectable families.'

'Because that would injure your chances of making this respectable business merger marriage you have your heart set on?'

'Exactly.'

She might not agree with what he planned to do, but her approval was neither necessary nor of any consequence. In twelve months' time she would return to Australia while he had every intention of doing all he could to correct the mistakes of the past.

'As much as I would like to retire from the social scene for a few months, I cannot avoid it entirely. There are at least half a dozen events I must attend if I'm to not give grave offence to my associates.' He had a vision of redeeming the

Vieri name and he wouldn't let all his hard work be undone by a broken engagement.

Monique glanced towards the back of the plane and her expression told him she was thinking of her niece. When her gaze found his again, he knew she was thinking about how much she owed him. 'What you need, Luca, is a plus one.'

'I do not know what this means.'

'A woman you trust—a friend or a cousin maybe—who'll accompany you to all these parties and dinners you have to attend, but who won't get the wrong idea, who knows you're not interested romantically. In an ideal world, she'd be a woman all of your associates would realise you're not serious about too, which is why a family member or long-standing friend would be perfect. The way these things usually work is that you also act as her plus one—attend events with her so she doesn't need to go alone. A reciprocal arrangement.'

Everything about this woman intrigued him. 'You have had an arrangement like this with someone in the past?'

She shrugged. 'Sure.'

Why had she needed this plus one? And who had he been?

'A plus one can also act as a watchdog—prevent any other woman from trying to monopolise your time or make a move on you. Though, to be honest, most women will back off when you have a date on your arm. So…problem solved.'

Her words made an alarming amount of sense. 'You make a compelling case for this plus one arrangement.'

She tapped her fingers against those delectable lips. 'What would be perfect is if you could find someone that Signor Romano instinctively knows you're not serious about. That would help to soothe his pride. I imagine he's not a man who would like to think his daughter could be replaced so easily.' She stared at him expectantly. 'Does anyone spring to mind?'

Everything inside of him tightened. There was one woman who fitted that description perfectly. *Monique.*

There had to be a hundred reasons against it, though. He needed to think. Ignoring the thundering of his heart, he nodded. 'I will put my thinking cap on. You have given me much to ponder. Thank you, Monique. And now you should try to get some sleep. It's getting late.'

Without another word, Monique moved back to her own seat. He should follow his own advice and try to sleep. Instead, he kept turning her suggestion over and over in his mind. Monique Thomas as his plus one? It could be the solution he'd been searching for.

The Villa Vieri was… Monique gulped. It was the size of a palace!

'I currently live in this wing of the house. It is

where Benito, you and Fern will also be established. The housekeeper will show you to your quarters shortly, but first I wanted to show you this.'

Luca led them through a series of unbelievably grand rooms—all generously proportioned and opulent. He carried Benny in one arm, as if it were the most natural thing in the world. Benny, who'd grown used to his father, reached up to pat Luca's cheek and tried to reach for a lock of his father's hair. Monique sympathised with the child's fascination. She found herself staring at Luca's hair all too frequently too, wondering if it'd be as soft and springy as it promised. Luca turned his head at his son's touch and pressed an absentminded kiss to his son's hand. The caress made her stomach turn over.

He threw open a set of French doors and then gestured at the view spread before them. 'This is the garden.'

Her jaw dropped.

He chuckled. 'It will do, yes?'

'Oh!' It was all she could manage.

'You might not be able to take the children to the park to play, but I think you can see that might not be as necessary as you once thought.'

'How big is it?' she breathed.

'Only two point four hectares.'

*Only?* She'd had no idea one could actually have an estate in the middle of Rome, but it was clear that was exactly what the Vieris had. As they'd driven through the black wrought-iron gates at the front of the property, they'd been greeted with an avenue of clipped pencil pines and formal rose gardens with a spectacular fountain as a centrepiece.

Thorns and water? It'd made her shudder. Talk about disastrous for small children. She'd crossed her fingers there'd be a scrap of lawn out the back.

A scrap of lawn? She started to laugh. Spread before her, besides a paved terrace and cobbled paths, were grassy terraced lawns and mature trees. The children could run and play to their heart's content. Not that Benny was even walking yet, but it wouldn't be long. She imagined games of football and cricket…they could even fly a kite.

Off to one side was a wilder area planted with fruit trees, perfect for climbing, and flowering shrubs, perfect for hiding behind during a game of hide and seek. 'Oh, Luca.' She clasped her hands together. 'This is wonderful…perfect.' Her smile widened. 'My concerns must've made you laugh yourself silly.'

'A little,' he allowed with one of his rare smiles.

'There you are, Luca! So kind of you to finally grace us with your presence.'

Monique spun around to find a thin, exquisitely groomed woman marching towards them.

'Hello, Mother.'

He kissed the proffered cheek. When the

woman turned disdainful eyes to Monique, Fern pressed in close against her legs. Monique brushed a hand over the little girl's hair, resting it there as reassurance.

'Mother, this is Monique Thomas, Benito's godmother. She has kindly agreed to be Benito's nanny for the next twelve months. Monique, my mother Signora Conti.'

'How do you do, Signora Conti?' Monique dutifully managed.

The older woman didn't deign to reply.

'And this is your grandson, Benito.'

The older woman cast a critical eye over the baby and gave an audible sniff. 'At least he's not an ugly child.'

What on earth...? *Seriously?* Every muscle in Monique's body stiffened. That's all Benito's grandmother had to say on meeting the newest member of her family? Her heart started to burn. *This* was Luca's mother? She thought of the little boy he must've once been and wanted to weep for him. Children deserved to be cherished and made to feel loved. Signora Conti didn't look as if she'd ever loved anyone.

'Your father and I demand a meeting with you immediately to discuss the Romano situation. Bella can still be brought to heel with a few judicious assurances.'

'That's not going to happen, Mother.' He handed Benito to Monique, before introducing her to the housekeeper hovering nearby. 'Maria will show you to your quarters. Go and settle in the children. I will come and find you later.'

She didn't say anything, merely nodded. There didn't seem to be anything to say. But he looked so suddenly worn out that she sent him a brief but heartfelt smile. One that she hoped told him she was on his side…and reminded him that while many burdens rested on his shoulders, there was now the delight of Benny in his life too.

Maybe it was fanciful to hope a simple smile could say so much, but she fancied his expression lightened.

She followed Maria back through the house and up a grand staircase, introducing her to the children as they went. The delight in her eyes when they rested on Benny told her all she needed to know.

Fern tugged on her hand. 'Tell me the story,' she whispered, gnawing on her lip as she stared around the vast house.

Monique silently asked if Maria would like to take Benny—an offer that was instantly and enthusiastically accepted. The housekeeper had him chortling before they'd taken another three steps.

'Once upon a time,' Monique started, swinging Fern onto her hip, 'Princess Fern went on an adventure with her friend, Prince Benny. They travelled across oceans to a faraway land to stay in a palace with a beautiful garden.'

It was a story she'd started days before to prepare Fern for the imminent changes about to happen in their lives.

'When they reached the palace, Princess Fern met a fairy godmother called Maria, who loves children and is the keeper of the cookie jar.'

Maria chuckled and Fern's eyes lit up. 'Cookies?'

Monique nodded gravely. 'I think cookies might feature in the adventures of Princess Fern and Prince Benny.'

Fern rested her head against Monique's shoulder and the little girl's implicit trust had Monique's heart swelling and her throat thickening. She'd do everything in her power to give Fern all the love and security she craved.

As they walked up another set of stairs at the end of the corridor to the third floor, she explained to Maria that she was Benny's godmother and that she'd been a friend of his mother.

The housekeeper clicked her tongue. 'You do not have to explain why Luca—Signor Vieri— has hired you. We do not question *his* decisions.'

But she did those of other members of his family?

'I wanted you to know,' she said when they stopped at a door, 'I've no doubt you and other members of the staff here will love Benny and have his best interests at heart. It's therefore right that you know these things. Also, I may need your help.'

'Help?'

'I'll be here for twelve months, to give Benny some continuity, before returning to Australia. Luca—Mr Vieri—has asked me to train two nannies who will eventually take over my duties. Word of mouth recommendations would be very welcome.'

The older woman nodded. '*Sì*, this is something I can help with, Signorina Thomas.'

In that moment she knew she'd made a friend. 'Please, call me Monique.'

Monique didn't see Luca again until just before the children's bedtime. He played with Benny and Fern for a little, building a castle with them from wooden blocks, and making Fern laugh when he balanced one of her small soft toys on the top. He'd taken great pains with the little girl, and his patience and gentleness had won her over. The two of them had become fast friends.

Both children fell asleep as Monique read them a story. She put Fern to bed while Luca put Benny to bed.

'What do you think of your quarters?' he asked when they'd both returned to the nursery-cum-sitting room.

'They're wonderful.' And thankfully nowhere near as grand as the rest of the house, which meant she and the children could relax rather than worry about damaging anything.

The configuration was ridiculously convenient too. Off this main room a connecting door led to Benny's bedroom, with another connecting door beyond it that led to Monique's room, and then another after that to Fern's room. Each of the rooms also had a doorway to the corridor outside, but it meant Monique could leave each of the internal connecting doors open so she could hear if the children needed her during the night, so the likelihood of disturbing anyone else in the house was minimal.

'It's a great layout, Luca. The perfect set-up.'

He sipped the tea she'd made. 'You have made a big impression on Maria. She has been singing your praises.'

'I had a strategy before I arrived,' she confessed. 'I've lived in a close-knit community for a long time, so I know how someone new coming in can put people's noses out of joint. I didn't want your staff feeling slighted or overlooked for the role of nanny.'

He blinked as if the thought hadn't occurred to him.

'A harmonious environment will be best for everyone. And now that everyone knows my link to Benny and the fact that I'm only here for a year...' She trailed off with a shrug.

'*Dio!* You have thought much about this.'

'But of course.' Why should that surprise him? 'I promised to look after Benny to the best of my ability. This is me keeping that promise. I want to be an asset to you, Luca, not a liability.'

He stared. 'You truly mean that.'

Again, why should her words surprise him? 'After everything you've done for Fern and me, it's the least I can do.'

He shook his head. 'What I did for Fern... You owe me nothing for that.'

A fire stretched through the dark depths of Luca's eyes and it made her mouth dry. She forced herself to break eye contact. Her heart hammered in her ears. 'You're paying me a generous salary to anticipate any problems. I'm just doing my job.'

He straightened at the mention of her salary. 'I appreciate your foresight.'

While they were on the subject of potential problems... 'I wanted to ask if any members of your family are likely to come up to the nursery to visit Benny?'

He shook his head. 'I will take him downstairs some afternoons or early evenings so he can become acquainted with his wider family.'

She wanted to ask if she should anticipate any potential problems from that quarter—especially his mother—but his face had shuttered. She stared at the forbidding lines of his face that looked as if they were carved from granite and decided against any further probing.

*Asset, remember, not a liability.*

She clapped her hands lightly. 'Right, how soon would you like me to start training the nannies who'll eventually replace me?'

'Immediately.'

A spike of hurt pierced through her. He wanted to replace her so quickly? She tamped it down. 'Very well. How did you want to select the candidates? From an agency or would you like me to place an advertisement? And do you want to interview them, or would you like me to take care of that?' She bit her lip. 'I took the liberty of asking Maria if—'

'Yes, she told me.'

She tried not to wince. 'I'm sorry if that was out of line.' It hadn't occurred to her that he might consider it a liberty.

'Not at all. Maria has a niece, Anna, who is a maid here. She knows the family, is a hard worker, and her connection to her aunt indicates loyalty. She does not have formal qualifications but is willing to gain them if I wish it of her. She has many younger siblings so has experience with children.'

She tried to inject enthusiasm into her voice. 'She sounds perfect.'

He stared at her with those dark eyes and gave a nod to some silent question he'd seemed to ask himself. 'I would like you to have an assistant as soon as possible so you are not trapped here all the hours of the day.'

In her world, that's what being a parent meant. And she didn't consider it a *trap*.

'You are allowed some leisure time.'

And he'd like Benny to grow used to her occasional absences. She didn't know why that fact should prick her so painfully. It was a sensible thing to do.

'Perhaps you and Anna could select the second nanny together. I would like the two of them to get along.'

'Of course.'

'But there is no rush for that yet.'

He sent her a look that had all the fine hairs on her arms lifting.

'There is another reason I should like you to train Anna immediately. I have a favour to ask of you, Monique. If you agree, it means someone will need to tend to the children in your absence.'

Her absence? Of course she'd perform any favour he asked. Despite his protestations otherwise, she owed him so much. But... She swallowed. 'Will my absence be...prolonged?'

'No!' His eyebrows shot towards his hairline. 'It is not that kind of absence.' Something in his eyes gentled. 'I would not ask you to leave Fern for more than a few hours. Not at the moment when she needs to know you are near.'

Relief made her sag. 'Thank you.'

'The favour I have to ask of you will mostly take place when the children are asleep.'

She gulped. At night-time?

*Oh, don't go there, Monique. That's not what the man means.*

'It is you yourself who gave me the idea.'

Dear God. Had he sensed her attraction to him?

'A plus one for all of the events I need to attend. You were right. It is the perfect solution to my current dilemma.'

She willed her pulse to slow. What did the plus one thing have to do with her?

'You are the perfect candidate for such a role. Would you consider escorting me to the parties and receptions that I must attend during the next three months? I have whittled them down to only six. The others I can make excuses for. And I'm hoping that within three months I will have repaired most of the damage that has been done between Signor Romano and myself.'

She leaned towards him. 'You want *me* to be your plus one?'

'*Sì.*'

Those dark eyes bored into hers with an earnestness that had everything inside of her yearning towards him.

*In all the wrong ways.*

He nodded. 'Please, yes, I would like that very much.'

# CHAPTER FOUR

THOSE EXTRAORDINARY CARAMEL eyes turned almost golden in surprise at his request and Luca found himself holding his breath. It surprised him how much he wanted her to say yes.

She moistened her lips and nodded. 'Of course I will. I'll help in any way I can.'

All the muscles that had been clenched in painful anticipation of her answer loosened.

'But…'

The line of her throat bobbed and his muscles clenched hard and tight again. 'But?'

'Are you sure I'm the right person for the job?'

'You have reservations?'

'I'm not from your world, Luca. What if I let you down?' She rubbed a hand across her brow. 'I certainly don't have the wardrobe for it.'

That last was murmured almost to herself and he dismissed it with a wave of his hand. 'Your wardrobe will be taken care of.'

Actually, it would be nice to see her in something other than black and white. For some reason she persisted in wearing the same clothes she'd worn when working at the motel. She didn't need to wear a uniform while she was here. She was so full of colour on the inside it seemed a shame it wasn't reflected on the outside.

'I don't possess the polish or sophistication... or the *posture* of someone like your mother.' Her eyes widened as if his mother's posture was a thing of awe and wonder.

He was grateful she was none of those things. Monique had something much more valuable— sincerity.

The confusion suddenly cleared from her face and she clapped a hand to her chest. 'Of course! That's the point. It'll signal to all of your associates that our relationship isn't serious.'

He shook his head, smiling in spite of himself. 'You underestimate yourself, *cara*.' The endearment slipped out without his meaning it to. 'You have poise, but more importantly you have a natural warmth that will not ruffle feathers or raise hackles.'

She looked far from convinced by his words.

'Also, you will be perfect because you know what kind of marriage I intend to make and understand that your tenure in my household is temporary. I know you will not misinterpret the arrangement.'

She stared at him with those clear eyes. 'You mean I won't get the wrong idea and think our arrangement is in any way romantic…that I won't make the mistake of falling in love with you?'

She was beautiful this woman, and intelligent. And she took no offence at his words when other women would've thrown things at him. If things were different—

But they weren't.

He nodded.

'That at least is true,' she mused. 'I mean I *was* the one who gave you the idea in the first place.'

'And in return you get to attend several glittering society events that hopefully won't be too onerous.' He would do all he could to ensure she enjoyed herself.

Her lips twitched. 'Onerous? Seriously, Luca? Parties should be fun. I bet these ones will be too and if they're not, you're just not doing them right.'

She made him want to laugh. 'Then that is a yes?'

'Can you promise me champagne and caviar?'

'Only the finest.'

'Then, Luca, that is most definitely a yes.'

Luca glanced at his watch. He'd arranged to meet Monique in the foyer at eight o'clock sharp. He hadn't expected her to be late, but it was already ten minutes past the hour.

He paced for five minutes more before turning and taking the stairs two at a time. When he reached her door, voices sounded from behind it. One remonstrating—and as he didn't recognise the voice, he guessed it to be the dresser he'd hired—and the other more conciliatory. Monique. Her tone might be calm and even, but it had steel threaded beneath it. He tapped on the door.

It was flung open by Monique. One look at her and the breath snagged in his chest. *Dio mio!* In a gown of silk and gossamer she looked like a vision from a fairy tale. He'd only seen her in those sensible skirts and trousers paired with prim blouses, but this dress hugged her figure with the kind of loving care that made his mouth dry.

He'd not realised her waist was that tiny. Or that her breasts… The blood roared in his ears and heat stampeded through his veins. He swallowed and only just stopped himself from running a finger beneath the collar of his shirt. He forced his gaze away from those tantalising soft curves. 'You look a vision,' he managed, recalling his manners.

'Rubbish!'

He blinked. 'But the gown looks as if it were made specifically with you in mind.'

The dresser made a smug sound behind her. Monique glared at the ceiling and he could almost see her count to ten. 'It's not the dress I'm referring to. It's the most beautiful dress I've ever worn.'

He saw then that it didn't hide the burn scar on

her arm. He'd given that no thought. How insensitive of him! 'Would you be more comfortable in a dress with longer sleeves?'

'What?' She blinked. 'Oh, my scar? No that doesn't bother me at all.'

He was glad of it. She was beautiful as she was.

Her eyes suddenly narrowed. 'Does it bother you?'

'Not in the slightest.'

She searched his face with keen eyes, eventually releasing a breath and nodding. He sagged when she turned back to the dresser. 'Many thanks, *signora*, for your help, but I can take it from here. I wish you a very pleasant evening.'

When the dresser glanced at him, he gave a nod. They waited until she'd gathered her things and left.

Monique glanced down the corridor to make sure the woman had really gone and then hastened to her dressing table, pulling pins from her hair. 'That woman was an absolute tyrant.'

'What do you mean?'

She froze from where she surveyed her image in the mirror, a cotton pad halfway to her face as if to remove her make-up. Very slowly she turned on her chair. '*This* is how you want me to look?'

*Dio*. This was dangerous ground. 'What do you mean?'

She gestured to her face, her hair. 'This!'

He did his best not to scowl. She did not look as

warm and approachable as was her custom, but in his experience this was the way women liked to present themselves. Far be it from him to criticise.

'I don't look like myself at all! I hate looking so...'

He forced himself to remain in the doorway, painfully aware of the bed in the middle of the room. 'So...?'

'Fake and *plastic*.'

The breath she pulled in made her chest rise in the most intriguing manner, the action captured perfectly by the dress. Fantasies, hot and explicit, played through his mind. Fantasies of slowly removing that dress and kissing every inch of her body until she begged him for release. Of hearing his name on her lips and—

*Dio!* This was torture. He shook with the effort to remain where he was. Thankfully her attention had remained on her reflection and hadn't strayed to him. He let out a quiet breath.

'I'm not from your world, Luca, so I don't think I should try and look the part. Please give me ten minutes to make some adjustments. I'll meet you in the foyer as promised.'

She'd barely finished speaking before her fingers had gone to her hair to pull out more pins and undo the complicated hairstyle the dresser had created. Caramel hair fell down around her shoulders and all he could think of was running his hands through it and—

He turned and strode down the corridor as fast as he could.

Eight minutes later, she walked down the grand staircase and every pore of his skin tightened. 'Monique, you look magnificent!'

Pink flooded her cheeks, enchanting him almost as much as the caramel hair that curled around her shoulders. That, combined with the myriad colours of her dress—the lightest of champagnes through to golden ambers, with a darker pewter thread here and there—made it look as if the sun shone from within her.

'Magnificent,' he repeated as she came to a halt in front of him. The pink in her cheeks didn't subside and he curled his fingers into his palms to stop from reaching out and stroking a finger down the curve of her cheek.

She frowned. 'I'm not supposed to look magnificent. I'm supposed to look unsophisticated and unpolished…a little gauche, like I don't belong.'

She looked none of those things. She simply looked magnificent. He didn't have the heart to tell her that in removing much of her make-up and reapplying it in her own style, her complexion now looked dewy and fresh rather than flawless. Her eyes looked a tiny bit smoky and there was a hint of warm colour on her lips. In eschewing perfection she'd replaced it with a warm authenticity that was a hundred times more potent.

Every man who saw her tonight would want to worship at her feet. Rather than her protecting him from unwanted attentions, he'd be protecting her. For a moment he questioned the wisdom of this plus one arrangement. He wanted to turn her around and race her back up the stairs and hide her from the rest of the world.

It warred with other impulses, though. In eschewing the style currently adopted by his set, she revealed its limitations. And for some reason he found that heady. She deserved to be belle of the ball.

Her brow furrowed. 'Stop looking at me like that, Luca. It's just a pretty dress and some make-up. I don't know how any woman could help but be transformed by a dress like this.'

He wrestled his customary mask back into place, tucking her hand into the crook of his elbow and leading her towards the door and the waiting car. 'Do not sell yourself short, Monique. You are a beautiful woman. Never doubt that.'

She halted by the car. 'Are you sure about this? I wouldn't blame you if you were having second thoughts. There'd be no hard feelings.'

'Nervous?'

Her chin lifted. 'Not at all.'

'You still wish to help me?'

That chin lifted higher. 'Of course.'

'Then, no, I do not wish to turn back. You

will be my shield against a society that wants too much from me at the moment.'

'You want a lot from it too,' she murmured as she slipped inside the car.

That was true. He closed her door and strode around to the driver's side. 'For the foreseeable future,' he said, 'you will help me keep the peace. I am very grateful to you.'

'It's the least I could do.' The casual words were belied by the smile she sent him. 'Okay, now that *that's* settled, shall we embrace our roles and have fun?'

Fun? It wasn't a word he could recall applying to his life—duty, responsibility and hard work had usurped it.

*Parties should be fun.*

He shook his head. Parties were for networking, for showing off, jockeying for position, and wooing business associates. But he would do his best to ensure, for tonight at least, that this woman enjoyed herself.

As he expected, Monique made quite a stir among his peers when she walked into the party on his arm. Not that she noticed or had the least idea, which was an undeniable part of her charm.

He introduced her to his peers and business colleagues—people he'd grown up with and/or did business with. She greeted them all with her customary warmth. She didn't realise it, but the warmth she generated in return was also given to him by association.

It shocked him. He was used to respect, civility and a certain circumspection from his peers. Not warmth...or friendship. For the first time it occurred to him that his reserve and aloofness might have created a wall between him and the rest of the world.

The thought burrowed into him like a burr that couldn't be shaken. He pushed it away to consider later.

Glancing up, he found Signor Romano staring at him from the other side of the room. He touched Monique's arm. 'Bella's father is here. I must go and speak with him.'

Shrewd caramel eyes glanced up. 'I'll go and powder my nose before joining you.'

He appreciated her tact.

He threaded his way through the crowd to Signor Romano, and the two men shook hands, made small talk briefly before Signor Romano fired his opening salvo. 'This marriage between you and Bella can still take place, Luca. We—'

'I have too much respect for Bella to ask her to take on both me and a child when she's not ready for such a move.'

'She is a good girl. She will do as she's told.'

'She deserves to be happy, Erik.'

'You would make any woman happy.'

Bitterness momentarily twisted inside him.

His money and position would make any woman happy, that's what Erik Romano meant.

For no reason at all, Monique's face rose in his mind. His wealth and money didn't impress her. At least, not in that way. Winning her custody of Fern, that was what made her happy. Not wealth, position and a large staff at her command.

'And yet,' Erik continued, 'you will eventually marry. Some woman will become your son's stepmother.'

'Not, however, for the foreseeable future. I want to get to know my son first, build a relationship with him before allowing a third party into our lives. For the time being, Benito is my priority.'

'And yet it would appear my daughter has already been replaced in your affections.'

Luca wanted to swear at the mottled red that had crept up the older man's neck, at the furious flash of his eyes. This was exactly what he'd wanted to avoid.

'I'm sorry I took so long, Luca.'

Monique smoothly moved in to form a third in their party, creating a warm circle with her accompanying smile. She handed both men glasses of champagne. Immediately a waiter appeared at her elbow to proffer her a third glass. She smiled her thanks before extending her hand towards Erik. 'Signor Romano, yes? I am Monique Thomas.'

The older man blinked. 'You are... Australian?'

She turned reproachful eyes to Luca. 'You haven't told Signor Romano about me yet?'

He hadn't had a chance!

She turned back to the older man. 'I am Benny—Benito's—'

'Luca's son?'

She beamed at him as if delighted with him. 'Yes, Luca's son! I'm his godmother—I was a friend of his mother. I've come to Rome to help Benny make the transition. His temporary nanny, if you will. In return Luca has been kind enough to treat me to...*this*!' She gestured at the party. 'As a thank you. It's so terribly exciting.' Her eyes widened and she lifted her champagne flute. 'This champagne is a revelation,' she whispered.

And just like that she won Signor Romano over.

The woman was a witch. And a treasure.


'Thank you,' Luca murmured in her ear fifteen minutes later.

The touch of his breath against her ear lifted all the fine hairs on her nape. 'For?' She tried to keep her voice calm, but her pulse juddered and jammed.

'For smoothing things over with Signor Romano.'

She refused to glance up into those dark eyes. They were dangerous eyes that could mesmerise a woman…if that woman were stupid enough to let them. Monique might not have a tertiary education, but she wasn't that stupid.

She knew that with just a little encouragement from her she and Luca could become lovers. The idea sent sparks of electricity zapping across the surface of her skin. She'd recognised the male appreciation in his eyes when she'd opened her bedroom door to him earlier this evening. It was one of the reasons she'd removed her make-up—to remind him she wasn't from his world.

Only that appeared to have had the opposite effect!

Appreciation she could deal with. It had been the raw hunger that had flared in his eyes when she'd walked down the grand staircase towards him that had almost undone her.

*No!* She *would* resist. She'd seen what had happened when her mother and Skye had become mesmerised by men. It had always ended badly. She wasn't interested in perpetuating that cycle.

She glanced around at the party—at the crystal chandelier, the glittering lights and all the beautiful people. She felt like Cinderella at the ball with Luca as her Prince Charming. But that was a crazy lie she couldn't let herself believe for even a second.

She needed to stay rooted in reality. She'd be

grateful for what she had—Fern. She wouldn't crave anything more. She didn't *need* anything more.

She certainly wasn't going to give her heart to an emotionally unavailable man. That would only lead to heartbreak. She owed it to baby Benny to keep things in his new world stable, and she owed it to Fern. She pulled in a breath. She owed it to herself too.

'You smoothed things wonderfully,' Luca repeated.

Why didn't he sound happier, then? She glanced up. Why didn't he look happier?

'When you told him you and Fern would be returning to Australia in twelve months' time, it put his mind at rest.'

She couldn't see a hint of attraction or desire in his gaze now. Her fingernails curled into her palms. Her reminder of who and what she was had done the trick. She told herself she was glad of it. 'So what's wrong?'

'He still has hopes that Bella and I will make a match of it.'

He dragged a hand across his jaw and her mouth dried as she followed the action, imagined following it with her own hand and—

*Stop it.*

'How long do you plan to wait before you start…courting again?' Not that she could call anything so clinical and businesslike 'courting'.

'Not for six months at least.'

She made herself shrug. 'A lot can happen in six months. You've dispelled Signor Romano's fear that Bella can be replaced quickly and easily—he's maintained his pride—and you've bought Bella six months. Signor Romano's disappointment or Bella's inability to grow a spine and fight for the life she wants isn't your responsibility.'

He blinked and she winced, wondering if she'd gone too far, taken one liberty too many. Eventually, though, he nodded. 'That is true.'

He took too much onto his own shoulders. Mind you, those shoulders were deliciously broad, and his dinner jacket highlighted their breadth to perfection.

'It's just...'

She snapped back, closing her eyes and letting out a grateful breath when she realised he hadn't noticed the way she'd been staring at him. She forced her eyes open again and the expression on his face made her heart burn. 'It's just that you like him,' she finished for him.

'He's the kind of man I can look up to...in all the ways I'm unable to look up to my own father.'

He'd wanted Signor Romano as his father-in-law, but did he really think marrying Bella would've made him happy?

Did he even care about being happy?

The thought made her heart twist.

Sipping her champagne, she stared at the crowd. 'Are there any prospective candidates for your future wife here tonight?'

He nodded; his expression morose. 'Several.'

*Really?* 'Who?'

He bent his head to her ear and kept his voice low. 'See the woman in the dark blue dress beside the chocolate fountain?'

The chocolate fountain she'd ached to sample but hadn't, as she'd been too afraid she'd drip chocolate on her dress.

She studied the woman's face and then glanced up at him, wrinkling her nose. 'Really?'

'Why do you pull this face?'

'She was very rude to the attendant in the bathroom.' She'd had a bevy of lackeys she'd ordered about mercilessly with the kind of entitlement that had set Monique's teeth on edge. 'Unnecessarily so, I thought.' She couldn't imagine a woman like that having patience around small children. *Oh, Benny.*

'You did not like her manner?'

She didn't answer that. 'She's very beautiful and sophisticated, though. The two of you would look good together.'

He gazed bored into hers. 'But?'

'She'll be high maintenance, but maybe you won't mind that.' She paused. 'If you want a wife who has the same poise and polish—' and attitude '—as your mother, then she would be perfect.'

He stiffened. 'I do not like rudeness,' he murmured.

'No,' she agreed.

She made a vow then and there to discover as many of the names of Luca's potential brides as she could and to find out all she could about them…vet them if possible. Benny deserved a stepmother who loved him and would treat him well.

And Luca deserved the same from a wife. Even if he didn't realise it yet.

*Yes!* Monique grinned her excitement as she read the email. Her first lesson packet had arrived. She could start work on it tonight.

She and the children had been at the Villa Vieri for a fortnight now, and they'd fallen into an easy routine, but she was eager to get back to her studies.

She read through the instructions and then frowned. She'd need to print out a couple of things first. She tapped a finger to her lips, recalled Luca's huge home office downstairs that he used when he wasn't in his office in the city. It had a printer. Surely he wouldn't mind…

She copied the relevant material to a thumb drive and glanced at Anna, the nanny in training. Both children were currently down for their afternoon naps.

'Anna, do you mind if I pop downstairs to run

an errand?' She held up her thumb drive. 'I want to print off a couple of documents.'

'*Sì*, Monique.'

Monique tripped down the back stairs—the old servants' stairs, apparently. The soft soles of her shoes were silent on the polished marble tiles as she made her way through several large reception rooms on the ground floor to Luca's study.

She had no idea if he was working from home today, but the door was ajar. She knocked. When no one answered, she peeked inside. Empty.

She hesitated for only a moment. The printer was sitting right there, not being used, and it seemed a shame to waste the opportunity. She wasn't hurting anyone, and she was sure Luca wouldn't mind. Especially once he learned what it was for.

The first document had just finished printing and she was waiting for the second job to begin when Signora Conti, Luca's mother, slipped silently into the room and started towards Luca's desk. She swung around with a violent start when the printer started up again, clutching her chest as if to prevent her heart leaping from her body.

The minute she saw Monique, she drew herself up to her full height, her eyes flashing and chin lifting as she glared down her nose. Monique gulped. Her son had obviously inherited his height from his mother. When one coupled that with Signora Conti's ability to make one feel as if they were something disgusting on the bottom of her shoe, it meant she could do intimidation really well.

'I'm sorry, Signora Conti. I didn't mean to startle you.'

'What is the meaning of this?'

'The meaning of...' *um*... '...what?'

'What are doing. sneaking around in my son's office?'

'I'm not sneaking.' Her shoulders went back. 'I simply came in to print something. I—'

'Does my son know you are using his office?'

What on earth was she insinuating? That she'd come into Luca's office to steal something? She started to shake with the effort to hold her temper in check. 'I can assure you that Luca wouldn't mind me using his printer in the slightest.'

*Please, let that be true.*

'I believe I know my son better than some upstart foreign girl with dollar signs in her eyes and her gaze firmly fixed on the main prize of my son!'

*What?*

'And I'm going to disabuse you of such foolishness. I know all about you, Ms Thomas, and I know all about your friend Anita Lang too. Girls like you will stoop to any level to find an easy meal ticket, but in this instance—'

'You can say what you like about me.' Monique's voice shook. 'I don't care what you think of me. But you will not insult Benny's mother like that.'

'I—'

'Anita never used Benny as any kind of weapon or bargaining tool over your son, though she certainly could have. If she'd been after a meal ticket, as you call it, she had one. But she didn't cash it in. She was a kind, loving, honest person who'd have never acted without integrity. You have no right to denigrate her character.'

'You *dare* raise your voice to me?'

She wasn't kow-towing to this woman. She might've promised to do all she could to make Luca's life easier, but that didn't include letting anyone besmirch Anita's memory. 'You dare insult Benny's mother—a woman you never met?' she countered.

Luca entered the room, intent on the papers in his hand. He froze when he realised he wasn't alone, his gaze no doubt taking in the way Monique's chest rose and fell, along with his mother's heightened colour.

Signora Conti lifted her chin. 'This girl is not to be trusted, Luca. I found her sneaking around in here.'

If he gave credence for one moment to his mother's assertion…

He raised an eyebrow, and Monique gulped

again. He could do supercilious with the best of them.

'I find that hard to believe, Mother.'

He glanced at Monique. This time his raised eyebrow was encouraging rather than cutting. She drew in a breath and made sure to keep her tone even. 'I came down to print off a couple of things.'

When he held out a hand for the pages she grasped, she gave them to him without hesitation. She couldn't read the expression in his eyes when he handed them back, but she swore warmth momentarily flickered there. Warmth and approval.

'Monique has my permission to use the printer any time she wishes.'

She wanted to hug him.

'But that isn't all,' his mother continued. 'The *impertinent* girl was rude to me. I demand—'

'I find that hard to believe, but if Monique *was* rude to you…' he strode behind his desk and set his papers down, as if already bored with his mother's tantrum '… I dare say it was not unprovoked.'

The tightness binding her unravelled in a rush. She'd known he wouldn't be unfair.

'Luca!' his mother gasped.

Monique wanted nothing more than to sidle out of the room, except Signora Conti stood between her and the door. She'd never get out unobserved.

'What are *you* doing in my office, Mother?'

The deceptively quiet question had Monique swallowing. She turned back to the printer to gather up the rest of her pages, doing all she could to distance herself from the scene.

'I came to have lunch with you. It is not unheard of for a mother to want to spend time with her son.'

'Lunch was two hours ago.'

'But I know how often you skip lunch.'

Did he? He hadn't in Mirror Glass Bay.

'Your concern is touching,' he said with a dry drawl. 'Why did you not ring me first?'

'Because you have a habit of not taking my calls. Forget it, Luca. I have changed my mind.'

With that she whirled from the room. The silence she left behind was only punctuated by the sharp sound of her spiky heels receding as she stalked away.

Monique blew out a breath, rueful as she met Luca's dark-eyed gaze. 'I'm sorry. I didn't mean to cause trouble.'

'My mother?' His brows shot up. 'She is not trouble of your making, Monique.' He tapped a pen against his fingers. 'Did you walk in on her or she on you?

'She on me.'

'I see.'

And then so did Monique. She smoothed a hand down her shirt. 'I'd just finished my first printing job, so it was quiet when she entered. At

# CHAPTER FIVE

IT WASN'T MONIQUE'S place to ask Luca what he thought his mother was up to. If he wanted to confide in her…that was a different thing. *Asset, remember, not a liability.* Asking awkward questions wasn't part of the remit.

She shifted her weigh from one foot to the other. 'Thank you for…'

'For?'

'Sticking up for me. I didn't think you'd mind me using your printer, but I should've asked first. I'm sorry. It won't happen again.

He shook his head. 'I trust you. You're free to use the printer whenever you need to.' The pen tapped against his fingers again. 'One final thing… The door to my office was unlocked?'

'It was ajar.'

His mouth thinned. 'I see.'

Was it supposed to be locked? Her heart thump-thumped as she stared up at him. With his olive skin, black hair and eyes fringed in silky dark first she didn't see me.' She moistened her lips. 'The sound of the printer gave her quite a scare.'

His gaze sharpened. 'Could you tell what she was making for—my desk or the filing cabinet?'

'It could've been either, but I think your desk.'

He nodded. 'Thank you.'

Dear Lord. What exactly did he think his mother was up to?

lashes, he should look like the Prince of Darkness. But he didn't. He looked…

She searched her mind for the right description. Like a hero? Like a dark-haired statue of David? Like an aristocrat stepping from the pages of a historical novel?

Yes, to all of those. But he also looked like a flesh-and-blood man with too many cares…who needed more sleep…who needed to laugh.

It hit her then, the description she was searching for. While Luca might be as attractively tempting as sin itself, unlike the Prince of Darkness he didn't scare her, neither did he threaten her. It was her own wayward desires that did that.

Luca was undoubtedly a powerful man, but every instinct she had, and the knowledge she'd gained from watching him with his son, told her he would never use that power for ugly purposes. Unlike his mother, he didn't treat those with less money and power as his inferiors.

When she'd said he didn't frighten her, though, it's not precisely that he made her feel safe—he upset her peace of mind too much for that. But she trusted him. She trusted he would never treat her unfairly.

Growing up as she had, she knew what a boon that was.

'You are staring at me, Monique, with the most

inexplicable expression on your face. What is it you are thinking, I wonder?'

She snapped back to the present. 'Oh, I...' Heat flooded her cheeks.

Giving herself a brisk shake, she tried to smile. 'Ever since I was fifteen, I've worked in the hospitality industry. Which means I've had a lot of different bosses with...different leadership styles—some less than ideal, some good, and some fabulous. Eve and Cassidy fall into that latter group. They have high expectations but in return they provide their staff with every support. You, Luca, are like Eve and Cassidy.' She smiled into stunned eyes. 'And that is a very good thing.'

Amusement lit his face briefly. 'All this because I stuck up for you to my mother?'

'No.' Her smile became genuine. 'You had every right to rake me over the coals, but you held fire until you had all the facts. You decided, based on what you know of me so far, to believe the best rather than the worst.'

His lips twisted. 'While I did the opposite with my mother.'

She hesitated. 'I suspect you based your reaction to her on all of your history together and your past interactions. You've nothing to feel guilty about.'

But his relationship with his mother was none of her business. 'I should get back upstairs before the children wake.' She held up her printed pages. 'Thank you for this.'

'You are studying?'

She'd started for the door but halted and turned back. 'An Associate Diploma in Childcare. I started it four years ago, but...' She shrugged. 'I hope to have it completed by the end of the year.'

Another thought occurred to her. 'I promise it'll have no impact on my duties here. I—'

'Of course it will. For the better. The fact you're studying is admirable. I will organise for a printer to be sent up to your room for your personal use.'

'That's very generous.'

His brows drew together. 'Would you like your own dedicated study? That could be arranged and—'

She found herself laughing. 'Thank you, Luca, but there's no need. I'll be happy to steal a couple of hours in my room when the children are sleeping. But thank you.'

She hesitated on the threshold.

'There is something else?'

Would he think it silly? No, surely not... He'd be delighted, wouldn't he? 'Benny said "Da-Da" this morning, clear as day.'

His mouth dropped open. 'He did?'

And then his entire face lit up, and she wanted to laugh for the sheer joy of it. She tried to shrug, tried to be casual, but she suspected he saw through her pretence. 'I haven't heard him say it before, and I thought you'd like to know.'

'He begins to know me.'

'He begins to love and look for you,' she corrected.

And then she left before she could do something silly, like kiss him.

'So tell me about this course you are doing.'

She and Luca were sitting in the nursery, sharing a pot of tea that Maria had brought up to them—ostensibly to help them unwind after the mayhem of bath and bedtime with the children, but in reality Monique suspected it was so she could have cuddles with them. Benny adored the older woman, and she and Fern had become the best of friends.

All was quiet now, though, and Monique sipped her tea gratefully. 'What would you like to know?'

'Why childcare? Have you always wanted to work with children?'

'I... Yes. I've always liked children.' She felt suddenly self-conscious under that steady gaze. 'I seem to have a knack with them.'

'That is evident.'

'I enjoy spending time with them. I—'

She broke off.

'You?'

She frowned. 'If I tell you the real reason, I don't want you feeling sorry for me. I don't want your pity. While I wouldn't have chosen the childhood I had, it is what it is. And I like my life now. A lot.'

His brows lifted. 'Then I certainly promise not to feel sorry for you.'

She loved the slight formality of his speech, and the accompanying seriousness. 'Excellent.' She sent him her biggest smile, before sobering again. 'Given my childhood, there weren't many options open to me in terms of furthering my education.' She'd managed to complete her schooling, which was more than Skye had done, but… 'University was out of the question.'

'A scholarship wasn't possible?'

'My grades were good, but not that good.' What with her part-time jobs and trying to look after Skye, there'd been little time for study. 'Neither did I want to leave town at that time.'

Understanding dawned in those beautiful eyes. 'You didn't want to leave your sister.'

She gave a half-shrug. 'So I kept my dreams small. I worked as a waitress, did a stint as a short-order cook, did housekeeping work in motels, and worked as an assistant in a childcare centre. That's when I decided to work towards my childcare qualifications.'

'So is this…' he gestured around the room '… the kind of work you would like to do?'

'No.' And then she realised how that must

sound to him. 'I don't mean I'm not enjoying this. I've loved every minute so far.'

'But it is not the dream.'

In hindsight, his understanding shouldn't surprise her. She wondered what his dream was. 'It's full-time work, the salary will allow me to build up a nice little nest egg, and it's giving me the chance to finish my studies. All while giving me the opportunity to build a relationship with my godson that will last a lifetime. I'm very grateful for this job, Luca.'

'And I am grateful you accepted it.'

She laughed, 'Listen to us being each other's personal cheer squad.'

His eyes warmed. 'I like this analogy.' His eyes became serious again. 'Now tell me about the dream.'

She stared into her teacup. 'The *dream* dream is probably out of reach, but one day I'd love to open my own childcare centre in Mirror Glass Bay.' She glanced up. 'The dream I'm working towards is opening a crèche at the Mirror Glass Bay Motel in the high season.'

'While working as a maid in the low season?'

She nodded.

'Eve and Cassidy…they are amenable to this idea?'

'Very.'

She couldn't read the thoughts racing behind his eyes.

Before she could ask him what his dream was, he said, 'This knack you have with children, how did you acquire it? Was it something you were born with—an innate talent—or is it something that can be learned?'

She almost said she didn't know, but the dark intensity of his eyes stopped her. Her answer obviously mattered to him, so she forced herself to think hard about the question, reminding herself how he'd leapt to her defence earlier against his mother.

It occurred to her that, regardless of her gratitude or anything that had happened between them, she'd tell this man anything he wanted to know. No questions asked.

He leaned towards her. 'My question makes you sad?'

'What? *No!*' She tried to laugh it off. 'As I've told you, I was very involved from the moment my sister Skye was born. My mother, being the woman she is, didn't much take to parenthood. As a result, I grew very protective of Skye. And I guess I just learned from trial and error. Hence the knack I now have with children.'

His eyes burned into hers and the lines around his mouth deepened. 'What went wrong? What happened to cause a rift between you and your sister? Why does she not worship the ground you walk on?'

She stared up at the ceiling for a few moments,

before dragging her gaze back to his. 'My mother happened.'

She could still recall the precise moment she'd lost her little sister to her mother's influence with the same painful clarity today as she had eight years ago at the age of nineteen.

Skye and her mother had been sitting on the sofa as Monique had rushed around getting ready for her waitressing shift that evening. 'The lasagne will be ready in forty minutes,' she told them. 'I've set the timer.'

Her mother snorted, already onto her third can of bourbon and Coke. 'Look at Little Miss Goody-Two-Shoes in her maxi skirt and the buttons on her blouse done up to her throat.' She nudged Skye's arm. 'God forbid that one should show any flesh, honey.'

Her mother's mockery had been too much of a constant in Monique's life for it to have much of an effect. She'd spent a lifetime pushing away the pain caused by her mother's insults and criticism, so any hurt she felt now was quickly dispensed with.

She glanced at Skye, who refused to meet her eyes. She knew their mother's attempts to make her an accomplice made Skye uncomfortable. *Oh, honey, I don't blame you.*

She continued getting ready for her shift, making sure all her money was in her handbag, before slinging it over her body crosswise so she couldn't accidentally put it down and have her mother pounce on it and take all the cash.

Or her ATM card. Monique made sure to change the pin number on that regularly. In another couple of months she'd have enough saved to cover the bond on a little place just for her and Skye, far away from her mother's drinking and relentless procession of men.

'What do you think, honey?' Sharlene Thomas persisted.

'It's a bit old-fashioned,' Skye allowed.

'Positively Victorian!'

Her mother rolled her eyes before offering her fifteen-year-old daughter a cigarette. Monique froze. She met Skye's gaze and shook her head. Skye lifted a defiant chin and accepted the cigarette. She lit it, dragged deeply, and then puffed out an insolent stream of smoke—controlled and practised.

When had Skye started to smoke?

'Not a push-up bra in that one's arsenal,' Skye said with a cruel laugh, making her mother cackle. She turned back to Monique. 'Lend us twenty, Mon?'

It hadn't been her mother raiding her purse, but Skye. It was the insolent eyebrow lift that told her. Skye *wanted* her to know.

And *that* was the moment Monique had lost her little sister. She'd fought against it, of course. For months. But Skye had shifted her allegiance to their mother and there wasn't a single damn thing Monique could do about it.

She'd forced herself to keep her chin high, had forced the tears back and refused to acknowledge the chasm that had opened in her chest as she'd fished out a ten-dollar note. It had been all she could afford. 'This is the last time I give you money, Skye. If you want pocket money you'll have to ask Mum for it. Or I can get you some weekend shifts at the restaurant.'

Her sister had blinked, evidently not having foreseen this eventuality. Had she thought Monique had no backbone at all? She wasn't giving her sister money to waste on cigarettes and alcohol.

'I hate you Mon. You know that? So prim and proper and *good*. Maybe if you lightened up once in a while... But you don't have a clue how to have a good time. Well, you're not going to stop me from having one.'

Vicious, casual, cruel...and she probably hadn't meant it. But those words had sucked all that had been light and good from Monique's world. 'I have to go or I'll be late. Don't forget the lasagne.'

Luca stared at the devastation stretching through Monique's caramel eyes and wanted to swear, to smash something, to defeat those demons like some gallant knight of old. This lovely warm woman had poured her heart and soul into her sister's care. How could Skye have abandoned her so callously?

Because that's what Monique's poorly concealed devastation revealed—that Skye had repaid her sister's love and care with betrayal.

'What do you mean, your mother *happened*? I did not think she was interested in her children.'

Monique shook herself, sent him a smile that made his heart break a little. 'She wasn't interested in the responsibilities or practicalities of parenthood, but when Skye was fifteen it seemed to amuse her to turn Skye into her best friend… turn her into a mini-me. She encouraged her to smoke and drink, to skip school.

*Cavolo.*

'Of course, I couldn't compete with that. I was the person who nagged her to eat her vegetables and do her homework…keep her room tidy and help with household chores.'

He knew without being told that Monique had continued to keep her little sister fed and clothed. She'd probably paid all the household bills too.

'But I was, quote, "only her sister" and I couldn't tell her what to do.' She stared at her hands. 'She'd always craved our mother's love and attention, and while I know she loved me too, the lure of our mother's approval was too hard for her to resist.'

'But you didn't abandon her.'

'I stayed until she turned eighteen. But I didn't

have the stomach to watch her destroy her life. A school friend… Anita, actually…told me that the Mirror Glass Bay Motel was recruiting. I applied, was hired, and so I moved there and started a new life. It meant I was close enough in case of an emergency, but far enough away that…' She shrugged and didn't finish the sentence.

She didn't have to. What a big heart this woman had. Despite her sister's betrayal, she was prepared to risk her heart all over again now with Fern.

'With the benefit of hindsight, I realise I should've alerted the authorities to our situation.'

'You were only a child.'

'I was afraid they'd take Skye away from me.'

A fear no doubt reinforced by her mother. 'You were only a child,' he repeated.

'If I'd acted less selfishly, maybe Skye wouldn't have become addicted to drugs.'

'Or maybe it wouldn't have made any difference whatsoever. You are not the guilty party here, Monique.'

She brushed a hand across her eyes. 'I know. These are regrets, not a guilty conscience. But…' she met his gaze '…it's why I refused to take a chance with Fern's welfare.'

'I admire you.'

'Don't be silly. I'm only doing what anyone else—'

'And I am sorry for unearthing such painful

memories. It was insensitive of me and not my intention.'

She frowned. 'What *was* your intention?'

It was his turn to shrug. 'I wanted to know how you learned to relate to children so well in an attempt to copy you.'

Her eyes widened and she let slip a laugh. 'Oh, Luca, you goose!'

He blinked. No one had ever called him a goose before, and certainly not in a tone of such affection.

'You don't need to learn anything new. You already have it inside you. Benny's face lights up whenever he sees you. Plus, you've been so kind to Fern, so patient in winning her over.'

He'd made sure to be even-handed with the children. If he brought a treat to the nursery for Benito, he made sure to bring one for Fern too. It only seemed fair. Her wide-eyed surprise and hesitant smiles were ample reward.

Monique's niece was a gentle soul—a little shy and withdrawn, but clever too and with a cheeky sense of humour that delighted him. As soon as she fully trusted her new life with her aunt, he didn't doubt the little girl would blossom.

'I am glad you think so, but…'

When he paused, she leaned towards him and gestured for him to continue.

'I want to be the best father I can be. It is what Benito deserves. I want to know how to do better. I want to know what I can improve.' While he couldn't make up to his son for the loss of his mother, he could do all he could to be what Benny needed.

Her gaze dropped and she shifted back in her seat. His stomach clenched, instinct telling him he wouldn't like her answer, but she merely shook her head. 'The world is full of compromises.'

'Yes, but you must have some thoughts on how I can become a better father.'

'You want my honest opinion?' Those clear eyes lifted. 'Then if you want to be a better father to Benny, you need to spend more time with him.'

He stiffened at the implicit criticism. From Monique, who had only ever looked at him as if he were a hero!

'When we were in Mirror Glass Bay, you spent almost every minute with him, only dialling into work when he napped or at night when he was asleep. The first week here in Rome you spent a lot of time with him—checking in on him in the morning, often putting in an appearance at lunchtime, and spending much of the evenings with him. This week there have been days when he's seen you for less than an hour.'

'I am a busy man.' He shot to his feet to pace around the room. 'I have many demands on my time.' He couldn't continue to neglect the work piling up on his desk.

'I know.' Her lips turned rueful. 'That's what I

meant by compromise. You're not the only parent who has had to negotiate the tricky conundrum of work time versus family time. There're a lot of parents who leave the house before their children are awake in the mornings and don't return until they're in bed in the evenings. Many parents, though, don't have a choice.'

He glanced around at her sharply. She thought he had a choice? He was in charge of a legacy that went back five generations. Even if he was prepared to abandon his birthright, the promise he'd made his grandfather meant he couldn't.

He slashed a hand through the air. 'You do not understand!'

'That's true enough.' She glanced in the direction of the children's rooms. 'But you're wrong if you think I don't understand compromise.'

He blew out a breath, tried to temper his sense of injury. 'Of course you do. Forgive me. That was unfair.'

Those clear eyes met his as if they saw him—truly saw him. It made his heart pound. Nobody had ever looked at him that way. Something inside him battled then to break free, but he forced it back within the boundaries he'd set for himself. But the effort had perspiration prickling his nape.

She shook her head, as if trying to shake herself free from some unwanted thought. 'I've no choice but to work, but you're insanely rich, Luca. You should be able to fashion the world to suit you.' Her brow wrinkled. 'But I can see you feel trapped. I'm just not sure by what.'

He straightened. 'I have a responsibility to the Vieri Corporation, to the Vieri name, to all the hard work the previous generations have carried out. It is my duty to honour and expand on their success.'

The furrow on her brow didn't clear. 'But you don't have to do it all on your own, do you? You have a large family. Surely the responsibility can be shared around? I can't believe every member of your family is as irresponsible as your parents, aunts and uncles. Why do you feel you must do it all on your own?'

Because there was a traitor in their midst, and he didn't know who he could trust.

But once he'd discovered the answer to that mystery, once he knew who he could trust, once calm and order had been restored, could he then rethink the company's internal structure?

'Luca, all any of us can do is try to be the best parents and the best role models for our children that we can be within our means and circumstances.'

The best parent he could be... Discovering he had a son had come as a huge shock and his only thought had been to race to his son's side to claim him as soon as possible. He hadn't thought beyond that or what came after. But now he had to decide what kind of parent he wanted to be.

One thing was certain. He didn't want to be the same kind of parent as his own mother and father—distant, remote, and bent more on their own pleasure and convenience than anything else.

He suddenly became conscious of the time. If she wanted to study…

He rose. 'It's getting late. You haven't forgotten the Gallineri party next Saturday night?'

'Of course not.'

It was a two-pronged affair—a select group of thirty for dinner followed by a lavish party for two hundred afterwards.

'I will have dresses sent over from several of the same fashion houses that Bella frequents. You can choose whatever you like. You'll need another four outfits as well, so—'

'I'd really rather you didn't.'

He blinked, wondering if he'd heard her right. She'd risen too and he tried to not notice the way the curves of her breasts pushed against the soft wool of her thin sweater.

He swallowed. 'Is there a different designer from whom you wish to procure your garments?'

'Heavens, no! The thing is, Luca, I don't want designer dresses. I don't want to sound ungrateful, but I'd rather choose outfits that reflect my true position here. I'm a visitor to your world. I should wear clothes that reflect that. It's a strategy that will allay any lingering doubts Signor Romano might have about me accompanying you to these events.' She bit her thumbnail. 'And hopefully signal to your associates that you're not ready to date yet, which will keep everyone else from feeling slighted. That's the whole point of me acting as your plus one after all.'

It was true, and her strategy was a sound one. His head could see the wisdom but something inside him resisted the reasoning. She should be dressed in the finest silks and laces. She'd looked an utter vision at the previous party.

'I'd like to buy clothes I can wear when I return to Australia.'

He stiffened. 'You will not be paying for these purchases. You would not be incurring such expenses if you were not doing this favour for me.'

He thought she might argue but eventually she surrendered with a nod. 'And to be honest,' she added, 'I'd feel much more at ease not wearing designer dresses.'

The smile she sent him had his skin tightening. She was so beautiful it wouldn't matter what she wore.

'I was so afraid of spilling something on the dress I wore at the last party I didn't eat a thing all night.'

'*Dio!* But you must've been ravenous by the time we got home.'

That made her laugh. 'Let's just say I had a *very* hearty breakfast the next morning.'

He took a step towards her, stretched out a hand

as if to touch her, a wave of tenderness nearly toppling him. Her quick intake of breath brought him back to himself and he forced his hand back to his side, the blood in his veins pounding so hard he felt bruised from the inside out. 'Please, Monique, you do not need to go hungry in this house.'

The thought of her going to bed hungry… It hurt something inside him. How often had she done that as a child? She did not have to do that here. 'You are free to use the kitchen, to make yourself whatever you want at any time. Promise me.'

If possible, her eyes grew even bigger. She swallowed and nodded. 'I promise.' She rubbed a hand across her chest. 'Thank you.'

What was she thanking him for? He should've noticed she'd not eaten. He should've taken better care of her!

Her brows drew together. 'Luca, I'm not in any danger of starving, you know.'

He tried to shake himself free from the confusion that had him in its grip. It was just…he'd given her her heart's desire. Her happiness and high regard were swiftly becoming addictive. He found himself wanting to repeat it again and again.

*Dangerous. Very dangerous.*

It was something he had to resist. To surrender to it would make a mockery of all his grandfather's hard work and all that he owed the older man.

'I would appreciate two further things from you, Luca.'

Anything. 'Name them.'

'The first is an afternoon off to go shopping.'

'You may arrange your work schedule any way you wish. I trust you with it implicitly.' She considered Benito's welfare as important as she did Fern's. As much as he did himself.

'And advice on where to shop. Something along the lines of a large department store…?'

A slow smile spread across his face. 'I know just the place. Is Wednesday convenient for you?' At her nod, he said, 'I will organise a credit card for your use, and a driver.'

'Oh, that's not necessary. I—'

She broke off with a laugh at whatever she saw in his face. 'Very well. Thank you. I appreciate it.'

He wondered what she would say when she discovered the department store he wished to take her to had once been the jewel in the Vieri empire's crown? His hands clenched. And it would be again.

He looked forward to the expression on her face when he told her. First, though, he must organise a snack from the kitchen for her. Never again was she going hungry on his watch.

# CHAPTER SIX

MONIQUE TRIED TO stifle the anticipation curling in her stomach as she skipped down the front steps of the villa to the waiting car. In the two and a half weeks she'd been here, she'd only left the estate to attend that party with Luca. But now she had an entire afternoon free.

If she did her shopping in record time, could she sneak in a couple of hours of sightseeing?

She hesitated, before sliding into the front passenger seat. 'I know I'm probably supposed to sit in the back, but I have a favour to ask and—' Her words tumbled to a halt when she glanced at the driver. 'Luca!'

He shrugged; his smile the kind that could slip beneath a woman's guard. 'I decided to play hooky from the office for the afternoon.'

He had? She tried to contain a surge of delight.

'But I have an ulterior motive for coming along.' He suddenly frowned. 'I did not think you would mind.'

'Of course I don't mind.' The breath had jammed

in her throat, making it hard to get the words out, making them breathless.

'What is this favour you were going to ask?'

'Oh, it was nothing. Nothing at all.' She didn't want him to think she was unhappy or unsatisfied with her position in his household. There'd be time to sightsee another day.

'Monique, I would wish—'

'I just felt wrong about sitting in the back, that's all. I'm not a member of your family and—'

'I consider you part of Benito's family.'

*Oh.* She tried to not let his words affect her. It didn't change the essential relationship between him and her. She sent him what she hoped was a cheerful smile as he drove out of the huge iron gates. 'The truth is one gets a better view sitting in the front.'

She couldn't see any landmarks that she knew, but when they crested the rise of a hill at the end of the road, Vatican City with St Peter's Basilica came into view in the distance and her breath left her on a whoosh. 'Look!' She pointed. 'It's as beautiful as I always imagined.'

'You must make time to visit it while you are here. It has a fascinating history.'

'And the ceiling of the Sistine Chapel?'

'Sublime.'

She sagged. She was tempted to pinch herself. Was she really in one of the most romantic cities in the world? This was the kind of thing that happened to other people, not her.

Luca seemed content to drive in silence, without conversation, but it wasn't the kind of silence that was unpleasant, and it gave her a chance to focus on the city unveiling itself before her in all of its complex beauty.

It no doubt gave Luca the chance to concentrate on negotiating the insane traffic!

Which he did with admirable ease.

'You must have nerves of steel,' she murmured when a van pulled out in front of them, only missing them by inches as a Vespa sped down one side of them in the impossibly tiny alley formed by the two lanes of traffic. How it didn't clip a side mirror she'd never know.

'One becomes accustomed to it.' His sudden smile sent her heart pitter-pattering. 'It's a little different from your sleepy Mirror Glass Bay, yes?'

That made her laugh, and then she gasped, looking beyond him. 'That's the…'

'Acropolis,' he supplied.

She could only nod in dumb stupefaction. 'But it's right here in the middle of the city.'

'*Sì*. You have to understand that Rome is an ancient city, and the modern city has sprung up around it—the old and new are blended together and live side by side. We are a city that embraces both our past and our future.'

'While relishing your present?'

Her question made him frown, as she'd meant it to. From where she was sitting, Luca was too intent on both the past and the future at the expense of his present. She didn't think that was any way to live.

*Be an asset, not a liability.*

She went back to gobbling up the view outside.

Luca broke the silence a short while later. 'This is our destination.'

He pointed to a grand seven-storey building in red brick. Its mullioned windows in their black frames and iron grillwork and big glass revolving doors gave it an understated elegance. Before she could make out its name, they'd descended to an underground car park, where Luca parked his car in a reserved bay.

'Come! Let us go purchase the things you need.'

She pushed out of the car before he could come around to open it for her. Luca was a gentleman, he observed all such niceties, but those kinds of niceties were wasted on the likes of her. And if she told herself that often enough, she might even start to believe it.

She stared at him over the car roof. 'You're coming shopping with me?' She'd thought he'd dash off to a meeting or to do business somewhere.

Something flickered in the backs of his eyes and a mask slid down over his face as he motioned her in the direction of the elevator. 'It had been my plan, but if you would prefer to shop alone then—'

'No! I just… Won't it bore you silly?'

'Why would you think that?'

They stepped into the waiting elevator. 'In my experience, men hate clothes shopping with women.'

A gleam lit his eyes as he punched in a number. 'That must be because they have not shopped at Gianni's.'

That was the name of the store?

'Gianni Vieri's, if one wants to give it its full name.'

'This is *your* store?'

Her mouth fell open and he laughed.

'Who was Gianni? Your grandfather?'

'Great-grandfather. This store was once the jewel in the Vieri crown.'

No sooner had the words left his lips than the elevator doors slid open to reveal rows of counters glittering with cosmetics and perfume, and she couldn't contain her happy sigh. Glass and brass twinkled and glowed in the warm overhead light from a series of opulent chandeliers. Even the air smelled expensive.

'The old décor has been kept.' She pressed a hand to her chest. 'I feel as if I've just stepped onto the set of an old movie.'

'*Sì*. It is part of its charm.'

'Oh, Luca, it's beautiful. I love it. And I guess you must too.'

'*Sì.*'

But the single word emerged tight and clipped, the lines bracketing his mouth deepening. 'Come, women's fashions are this way.'

'Oh, but first…'

He swung back to her.

'It's just…' She gestured to the perfume counter. 'We have to spritz something lovely on.' It's what she always did whenever she visited one of the big department stores in Brisbane. She couldn't afford French perfume, but on days like today she could spray a little on and relish the experience.

He laughed, his tension dissipating. 'Very well, lead the way.'

A woman at the perfume counter spritzed a brand-new perfume onto Monique's wrists and explained it had a top note of orchids followed by softer hints of jasmine and citrus.

She pronounced it heavenly and said she'd think about it, that she wasn't shopping for perfume today.

'You do not wish to buy it?'

She smiled at his perplexed expression. She couldn't justify the expense of French perfume, not that she had any intention of telling him that. 'You don't understand. Back home I so rarely get a chance to visit the city. So to come to a department store like this is a real treat. And traditionally I always begin such an excursion fortified with a spritz of something lovely. It just sets the tone and makes me feel...spoiled.'

He frowned. 'I see.'

He had no idea. 'Are you wearing cologne?' She leaned in close and sniffed, drawing a deep breath of him into her lungs. And then realised what she was doing.

She shot back as the scent of fresh soap and warm male skin assailed her senses. Stunned dark eyes met hers before he blinked his usual composure back into place. Dear God, what had she been thinking? *Act normal*. Maybe he wouldn't notice her reaction if she acted as if it were no big deal.

'Here.' She seized a nearby bottle of cologne. 'Try it. Put some on. It's fun to try something different.'

He blinked but did as she ordered. 'What do you think?'

He angled his neck towards her and her mouth dried. All she could think about was pressing her lips to the strong tanned column of his throat and running her hands around to the nape of his neck and—

*Stop it!*

She forced herself to lean in a little closer and take a cautious sniff. The warmth of amber and a hint of cardamom spiced the air. She closed her eyes in momentary appreciation.

'You approve?'

'Very much.'

She made herself smile. She made herself take a step back. But dark eyes met hers and their gazes held. Something arced between them—a silent male-female acknowledgement of attraction and…liking? It was the latter of those that gave her pause and made her heart hammer in her chest.

Not her liking him. He'd had her undying *like* from the moment he'd helped her rescue Fern. What she hadn't realised was that he might actually like her in return. As a person.

They dropped their gazes at the same time, and she wondered if her eyes were as troubled as his.

'So…' She clapped her hands and made a show of keeping things light—something that came as second nature to her. It was the strategy she'd used to keep Skye from getting too upset whenever their mother had stumbled home drunk to flake out on the sofa. 'Now that we're smelling gorgeous, we can embark on the shopping for real. And it looks like women's fashions are this way.'

Oddly enough, the tension between them evaporated when they started looking at dresses and pantsuits.

'That is horrible, no?' Luca said when she pulled out a heavily beaded navy concoction. 'It is for a much older woman. What about this one?'

'Those frills…' She grimaced. 'Too fussy.'

He put it back and pulled out another.

'Oh! That one's perfect.'

She'd never realised shopping with a man could be such fun. He gave his opinion with a decisiveness that made her laugh. They argued good-naturedly over the pros and cons of certain necklines and hemlines. She loved every moment of it.

She eventually settled on a beaded dress with a fitted bodice in the most glorious shade of jade, a simple silk sheath in a mouth-watering orange, and a butter-yellow trouser suit that hung like a dream. 'There, that's the upcoming events taken care of.'

He frowned. 'But we have another five parties to attend and you have only three outfits.'

'I can wear these more than once, Luca.'

'*Dio!* No. You must also take the rose-coloured velvet dress and that pretty red cocktail frock. Besides, there may be one or two additional events that come up at the last moment and it is best to be prepared.'

She wanted to argue with him. She'd never spent this much money on clothes in her entire life.

He gave directions to the saleswoman and then

turned back to her. 'Do not feel guilty,' he chided. 'All of these together are still less than that designer dress in whose service you starved yourself.'

*Gah! Don't tell me that.*

'So you see? You are saving me money!'

That made her laugh. 'Now you're spinning fairy stories. This—'

He pressed a finger to her lips. 'You are doing me a favour being my plus one and it is only right I ensure you have the equipment necessary to accomplish the assignment. *Sì?*'

Her mouth had gone dry at his touch, rendering her speechless, so she simply nodded.

'Good.'

He removed his fingers and she could breathe again. 'Luca, I can assure you it isn't a hardship attending parties with you.'

'I am glad to hear it.'

'It's fun.' She said the words deliberately, because fun didn't seem to feature on this man's radar at all and it broke her heart a little.

He blinked and stared as if he didn't know what to say. He had so much money and yet fun seemed a foreign concept to him. She sent him her biggest smile. 'Today has been fun.'

His lips relaxed into a smile. 'It has. But it is not yet over.'

He turned to the saleswoman, speaking in rapid Italian, and although she'd been learning the basics from Maria and Anna, she had no hope of following it.

It became clear, however, when a selection of shoes, purses and wraps were paraded for her appraisal. She chose a single pair of beige heels and a purse to match that would go with everything, deliberately hardening her heart against the crystal studded pale pink heels that were frivolous and totally unnecessary.

Luca spread his hands. 'You need more than one pair of shoes.'

'I have another pair at home. I don't need more than two pairs of evening shoes.'

He lifted his eyes heavenward. 'What am I to do with this woman?' He seized the pink heels and a matching purse and then a sumptuous faux fur wrap in white and added them to the pile. And then gave what sounded like another set of instructions to the waiting sales assistants—they now had three.

She frowned when pretty trousers, tops and capri pants were displayed for her inspection. 'Luca, I don't need any of these.'

'Please, choose a selection to humour me. I do not like all of the black and white you wear every day. It makes me feel as if you are working in a funeral home. It is most disconcerting.'

Her mouth fell open.

'It was your uniform when you worked as a maid and a waitress, and this I understand. But such a uniform is unnecessary when you are Benito's nanny.'

'Why?' It would be safer if they maintained the distinctions of their positions in his household. Those distinctions were in danger of blurring enough already due to their plus one arrangement.

'Because you are more than just a member of my staff.'

Her heart tried to dash its way out of her chest. She was more to him...?

'You have come to Rome out of the goodness of your heart because of your connection to Benito—because you love him.'

She gripped her hands together. Of course he meant her relationship to Benny. Nothing more. It'd be idiotic to think he meant anything else.

'His welfare and best interests are of primary concern to you. I think you love him almost as much as I do. And as his godmother you are family. As such, that makes us equals.'

The way he stared at her as he spoke invested his words with more meaning than he no doubt meant them to. She kept her hands pressed tightly at her waist and gave herself a stern lecture. Luca was outrageously generous, that was all.

*That was all.*

'So, please, choose five outfits that you can wear during the day. Outfits that are comfortable, practical and to your liking.'

She stared at the clothes he'd gestured to. All her working life it had been her role to fade into the background. Here Luca was asking her to stand out.

'This will be a sign to the rest of the household staff that where Benito is concerned your word is law, that you have my authority to make important decisions on his behalf.'

She glanced up. Perhaps not just to the household staff, but also his family? She sensed he didn't want her allowing his mother to walk all over her, though he didn't say that out loud. And she certainly didn't ask.

Without another word, she chose trousers, capris and skirts in the loveliest fabrics and a selection of tops—practical, colourful and pretty. 'I've never owned such beautiful clothes,' she said as they wound their way back down to the ground floor after Luca had organised for all the purchases to be delivered to the villa later that afternoon. 'Thank you, Luca.'

'You do not need to thank me. You need a working wardrobe while you are here, and I gave you no opportunity to arrange that before leaving Australia. We supply all our household staff with uniforms. This is no different.'

Except hers wasn't a uniform.

'Now, come, that's enough.' He halted in front of one of the large glass revolving doors. 'Tell me which of Rome's many sights you most wish to visit?' He glanced at his watch. 'We have several hours still at our disposal.'

She tried not to gape at him. Had he read her mind earlier? 'But…what about the business you said you had here?'

'It is completed.'

*She'd* been his business? She lifted her chin against the sinking of her heart. For all his pretty words earlier, he saw her as nothing more than another responsibility. Today's outing was merely another example of his innate generosity.

*What more do you want?*

It wasn't a question she dared answer.

'I may even tell you about it later. When we are sightseeing.'

She gnawed on her bottom lip, but he smiled—a true from-the-heart smile that had double the impact as one saw it so rarely—and she gave up worrying.

'I confess I find myself intrigued as to what you will choose.'

He looked as excited as a little child and she found it strangely endearing. 'You're going to find it horribly trite and touristy, I'm afraid.'

'I would be disappointed if it were not.'

She couldn't resist that smile. 'Okay, then the thing I most want…'

He leaned towards her. 'Yes?'

'Is to eat gelato by the Trevi Fountain.'

His mouth formed a perfect O, before he murmured something in Italian that made her want to close her eyes and purr. 'You are a remarkable woman, Monique.'

The way he said her name... *Dear Lord.*

'You could ask for the stars.' His rich chuckle filled the air. 'And yet all you want is gelato.'

'And the Trevi Fountain,' she reminded him. 'And it has to be *good* gelato.'

'Italy only does the best.'

She laughed at the way he straightened, as if he would fight any suggestion otherwise. 'Then we're in for a treat. The stars can wait until next week.'

Luca tried to not question too deeply his satisfaction when Monique's lids fluttered down over her eyes in appreciation as she sampled her first Italian gelato.

'This is delicious!'

If forced to guess her favourite flavour, he'd have said chocolate, but she'd pointed to a creamy passionfruit instead. Normally he'd choose a coffee-flavoured gelato, but not today. Today he'd selected a rich smooth caramel that coated his tongue in sweet promise.

Her eyes flew open, rooting him to the spot. 'Best gelato ever.'

He couldn't move, couldn't drag his gaze from those eyes, her smile or from the life that radiated from her every pore. As if aware of his scrutiny, as if the warmth of his gaze touched her skin, pink stained her cheeks.

He shook himself. 'I am glad it does not disappoint. And what of the fountain?' He gestured to the fountain in front of them. 'Does it too live up to expectation?'

'I think it magnificent. I need to pinch myself to believe I'm really here and that this isn't just a dream.'

She craned her neck, taking in all she could. As if trying to memorise every detail. He did his best not to notice the way her tongue touched the gelato or the shine it left on her lips. If he kissed her now, she'd taste cool and tangy and—

Not that he had any intention of doing any such thing!

*Sì*, she was beautiful, but a dalliance with Benito's godmother...? *Dio*, it would be very poor form indeed. Besides, he reminded himself, for as long as he continued to tread delicate ground with Signor Romano, he would not want whispers of any such liaison to reach the older man's ears.

If only those thoughts could dampen the tendrils of desire that curled around him with a gentle but insidious tyranny. He took a big bite of gelato, hoping it would give him brain freeze.

'The fountain and the square are both regal and charming,' Monique finally said. 'I suspect that might sum Rome up perfectly too.'

Except that was all conjecture on her part, and not based on experience. How could he have been so remiss and not shown her a little of what Rome had to offer before now? He'd kept her tied to the villa for the nearly three weeks. She must've felt as if she were under house arrest!

'You sum up my city perfectly.' He handed her a coin and gestured. 'You must, of course, toss a coin into the fountain to ensure you will one day return.'

Her fingers closed around the coin as if relishing the heat it had absorbed from his body. He gulped down more gelato.

Placing her back to the fountain and closing her eyes as if to make a wish, she threw the coin high into the air over her shoulder. It glittered in the sunlight as it turned over and over, landing in the pool with a splash.

He beamed at her. 'Now you will return.'

'I hope so.'

He would see to it. He wanted Benito to know his godmother, and to know her well, not just as a passing acquaintance. He wondered if she and Fern would consent to spend every Christmas with them.

He promptly lost his appetite. That would, of course, depend on his wife and what she wished to have happen at Christmas. Not that he could yet put a face to that elusive woman. It didn't change the fact that such a wife featured in his future.

'So?' She raised her eyebrows.

He raised his too. 'So?'

'You were going to tell me about your business at Gianni's today.'

Ah, that. Resolve settled in the pit of his stomach. Yes, it would be wise to tell her…and to remind himself of all he wanted to achieve. Leading her to one of the small tables that bordered the square, he held a chair out for her; taking the one opposite once she was seated. 'I wanted to walk the halls of Gianni's today as a customer. I wanted to try and see the store through your eyes.'

'Did you like what you saw?'

He nodded. He'd liked it very much.

She frowned as if something puzzled her. 'You're an important man, Luca, but hardly any of the staff seemed to know who you were. I expected… I don't know, more bowing and scraping, I suppose. As CEO I thought they'd roll out the red carpet for you. I mean, if you own the store you'd think—'

'But I don't.' Pain tightened his chest, making the words curter than he'd meant them to be. He tossed what was left of his gelato into a nearby bin.

'I beg your pardon?'

'The Vieri Corporation no longer owns Gianni's. One of the first things my mother and her siblings did when my grandfather retired five years ago was to sell it. Secretly and swiftly before any of the rest of us could do anything about it.'

She stared at him as if his words made no sense. 'But you said it had been the jewel in the Vieri crown. Surely that means…'

She trailed off with a gulp, looking as if she wished she'd held her tongue. He nodded. 'It should be cherished and honoured…kept safe.'

She nodded back warily, as if afraid she'd overstepped a boundary. Boundaries he should strengthen.

'It broke my grandfather's heart.'

She reached out as if to touch his hand, to offer comfort, but pulled back at the last minute. 'I'm sorry.'

She moistened her lips. He refused to allow his attention to linger on their soft curves or to allow the craving to taste them to grow. Monique was forbidden fruit. He would not be another weak-willed pleasure-seeking Vieri.

'Is your grandfather still alive?'

Her question made him smile. 'Very much so. He now lives on a small vineyard in Tuscany where he makes wine and tends his garden.' His grandfather had worked hard all of his life. He deserved a trouble-free retirement. He deserved to have both the Vieri name and Gianni's restored before he died.

'You sound fond of him.'

'My parents had very little time for me when I was a child, but my grandfather spent as much time as he could with me and my cousins—half-days and weekends. He would take us all to his beach house in summer for two weeks.' His grandfather was the only reason his childhood hadn't been a cold and lonely wasteland of privilege. 'I can see now how he fostered relationships between us cousins...so we would always have each other. In that way he gave us a sense of the true meaning of family.'

'He sounds like a fine man.' The look she sent him—warm but piercing—left him feeling suddenly naked. 'I think you must be like him.'

It was the greatest compliment anyone could pay him.

'I'm guessing you're modelling your parenting style on him rather than your parents.'

He was trying to, but... A grandfather's love and care did not make up for a parent's indifference. If he'd lived permanently with his grandfather things might've been different. But that hadn't been possible. His grandfather had been working hard to keep his ungrateful offspring out of trouble and out of debt.

Benito deserved better than a part-time father. Luca needed to find a way to balance his commitments to the Vieri Corporation with fatherhood.

*You don't need to do it all alone.*

Monique's words from earlier in the week

whispered through him. He wanted to believe them, but someone needed to be the head of the company. And his grandfather had chosen him.

He pulled in a slow breath and released it. 'My grandfather handed control of his share of the company to me after his offspring sold Gianni's. My cousins and I made a bid for power and ousted my uncle from his position as CEO. We have been working towards re-establishing the Vieri name ever since.'

'So you're all working together—you and your cousins?'

'*Sì.*'

She frowned. 'Then why do you feel so alone, feel as if you must do it all on your own?'

'Because one of my cousins is working against me, working with the previous generation to undermine my control. And I do not know who it is.'

'Which means you don't know who you can trust,' she said slowly, pressing a hand to her stomach as if the gelato she'd eaten now no longer agreed with her. 'Well, that sucks.'

Her bluntness surprised a laugh from him. '*Sì.* It does indeed, as you say, suck.'

'You'll get to the bottom of it. You're clever and determined.'

Her faith in his abilities touched him. Yes, he would get to the bottom of it, and he would make things right. But at what price?

'Luca?'

He glanced up at the question in her voice.
'Who owns Gianni's now?'

'Signor Romano.'

Her eyes widened. 'That's why you were going to marry Bella? Gianni's was…what? Part of her dowry?'

Her distaste was plain. 'It is how things are done in my world.'

'It seems so…cold-blooded.'

The hand he rested on the table clenched to a fist. When she glanced at it, he forced himself to relax it again. 'Cold-blooded would be to pressure Bella to go through with a marriage she does not want. Cold-blooded would be to marry a woman I do not like or respect. Cold-blooded would be to marry a woman who would not be kind to my son, simply because I want the respectability her name and family's backing will give me.'

He shook his head, but he wasn't sure who he was trying to convince—himself or Monique. 'I intend to honour and respect the woman I marry. While it might not be a love match, there will be affection, and I have every intention of honouring my marriage vows.'

She met his gaze. He knew he looked fierce and grim, but it didn't seem to frighten her. 'I'm sorry, you're right. It isn't cold-blooded. Not when you put it like that. You're a good man and I shouldn't have made such a snap judgement. As you say, our worlds are so different.'

He was no doubt violating ideals she considered sacrosanct and inviolable—like romantic love. He'd believe in that once too.

'When I was twenty, a woman I imagined myself in love with took money from my father to break up with me. It made me realise that while my wealth provides me with much privilege and a luxurious lifestyle, it also brings temptations and enticements to the people I associate with—envy and covetousness in some quarters too. It is better for me to be realistic about this and not indulge in romantic daydreams.'

Her face fell. 'That's awful.'

Seeing it through her eyes...it was all he could do not to flinch. 'I can, however, make a clear-eyed marriage with a woman I respect, a woman who will not tarnish the Vieri name. It is not a tragedy, Monique. Family is everything to my grandfather, my cousins and me. I will do all I can to make them proud. I will be more than content with that.'

'We're so different.' She managed a laugh and while it sounded genuine enough, he sensed the effort it cost her. 'I mean, you can trace your ancestors back at least five generations...probably more. While neither my sister nor I have the slightest idea who our fathers might be. To us, family feels like nothing more than an accident... a lottery...something to be overcome.'

Her family was the absolute antithesis of the

kind of family he needed to marry into, that his grandfather required he marry into, to save the family name.

Her face crumpled and for a moment he thought she might cry. *'Dio!'* He reached out a hand to her. 'What is the matter?'

'I should so wish Benny to marry for love rather than duty.'

Everything inside him protested at the idea. It would be otherwise for his son. Luca would make this sacrifice so Benito never had to.

That pretty chin lifted. 'I need to warn you that's what I'll be advising him to do, despite your thoughts on the matter.'

Her fierceness made him smile. 'It is what I wish for him too.'

Her eyes narrowed. 'As long as he falls in love with the right kind of woman?'

'No. If I make the right kind of marriage now, if I can fix the things that need fixing, Benny will not have to make any such sacrifice.'

With a funny sound—part-growl, part-groan— that was cut off before it could fully become one or the other, she covered her face with her hands.

He stared at her, nonplussed, before reaching over and tugging on one of her hands gently. 'I do not lie to you, Monique.'

'I know.' She lowered her hands, but his words had no effect on the unease swirling in her eyes. 'Will you explain something to me?'

He suspected Monique would champion his son to the ends of the earth. He'd explain anything he could to her. 'I will try, yes.'

'Can you tell me how this respectable marriage you plan to make will help you restore the Vieri name and reputation?'

'If you wish.'

'I'd like to understand.'

'Very well.'

'Would it be okay if we strolled as we talked?'

He felt the sudden restlessness in her as a similar restlessness stole over him. 'Come.' He stood. 'The Spanish Steps are this way. And from there we can walk to the Pantheon. Does that sound agreeable to you?'

'It sounds perfect.'

How he wished her smile would meet her eyes. Dragging a breath into cramped lungs, he tutored himself on keeping his voice calm and his heart steady. This was the path he had chosen, and while he might not be able to meet it with enthusiasm, he would meet it with grace.

He gestured the direction they should take and didn't speak again until they'd reached the Spanish Steps. She clasped her hands beneath her chin, and oohed and ahhed when she saw them, but not with the same fervour that she had the fountain they'd left behind.

'You ask how my marrying into one of the old,

respected families will help my family…and vice versa.'

She nodded.

'Currently there are companies that refuse to do business with the Vieri Corporation due to the previous leadership's…*unreliability.*'

Her quick glance told him she understood. Unreliability was merely a euphemism for his parents', aunts' and uncles' unscrupulous and at times dishonest business dealings.

'There are businesses I need to get onside, that I need to convince to work with me, if I am to take the Vieri Corporation into the future.'

She frowned up at him, and he took her elbow to guide her around a woman with a stroller who'd stopped in front of them.

'But if these businessmen know you, Luca, then they must realise you're honourable and reliable.'

'There's a difference between believing me honest and believing me capable of keeping power.'

A sigh whispered from her. 'I see.'

'In aligning myself with one of the big families, it will inject the Vieri name with a level of kudos and respectability I'd not be able to achieve any other way. It's an immediate endorsement from a respected source. While I might not yet have the trust of the wider business community, these big families do.'

'And in aligning yourself with one of them, their respectability and integrity will entice the businessmen you want to work with to trust you?'

'Exactly.'

'What does the old established family get in return?'

'Money. Their family estates are prohibitively expensive to maintain.'

She pursed her lips but remained uncharacteristically silent.

'I get the respectability I need while they get the money to maintain a family estate that goes back centuries.'

He watched her mull that over as they strolled along cobbled streets and past shop windows with enticing displays. He wasn't sure she saw any of it.

'Will marrying into one of these families help you counter the in-fighting in your family? Help you maintain control of the company?'

Every single one of her questions was on point. She might not have had as stellar an education as he, but she had a quick mind.

And a kind heart.

*'She has the kindest heart of anyone I know.'*

Cassidy's words to him in Mirror Glass Bay floated through his mind now, making his heart clench. If only Monique came from his world. If only—

He had to stop wishing for the impossible. It was his duty to focus only on what was necessary.

'Luca?'

He snapped back. 'The big families might not have the same wealth as a family like mine, but they have many contacts in both the industrial and political spheres. Those contacts will be of much assistance to me.'

'So that's a yes, then.' A tiny sigh puffed from her lips. 'How will it help you get Gianni's back?'

'Signor Romano has promised that if I can redeem the Vieri name, he will sell Gianni's back to me.'

She swung back to him. 'He knows the nitty-gritty of your plan?'

It was as if a cloud had passed over the sun. He glanced up but the sky was as blue as it had been earlier in the day. 'He is one of my grandfather's best friends. It is he and my grandfather who came up with this plan.'

'They *what*?'

'I trust them.'

'I can see that.'

'This plan...' he glanced down at her '...it is a sound one.'

Her sigh pierced all the sore places inside him, but then she slipped her hand into the crook of his elbow and he hugged that small warmth to himself.

'Thank you for explaining it all to me.'

'You are welcome.'

She gave a laugh. 'Wow, a family like mine would really be your worst nightmare, huh? Disreputable and constantly trying to extort more money out of you while giving supposedly in-depth reveals to the tabloids.'

Her words were irrefutable. He did his best to keep his shoulders back and his spine straight. Physically he and Monique might be close enough to touch, but in reality they couldn't be more distant from each other if they tried.

# CHAPTER SEVEN

MONIQUE SCANNED THE ballroom after returning from touching up her lipstick. She'd needed a moment to herself to gather the mantle of common sense and self-preservation around her again. She was starting to need such moments more and more frequently.

She'd taken such pains to create walls around her heart, to position each brick carefully and hammer it home with all the reasons she and Luca could never be more than friends. Yet one heated glanced from his dark eyes could have those walls cracking. And if she forgot to brace herself, one of his rare smiles had the potential to send them tumbling down until they were nothing but rubble at her feet.

She scanned the room for his tall frame, finding him easily—those broad shoulders standing out in the crowd and making her mouth dry with longing. Even in a crowd, his magnetism didn't pall.

*Stop it.*

She'd never allowed herself to dream for the impossible and she wasn't about to start now.

Skirting the edges of the crowd, she admired the women's dresses and jewels, the flowers and decorations that brought the room to sparkling life...the extraordinary champagne tower. It was all so wonderfully over the top she couldn't help but enjoy it.

But her gaze returned again and again to Luca, who stood with a group of other men, no doubt talking business. She knew he'd welcome her into the group immediately if she made her way over to him, but...

She pressed a hand to her stomach and swallowed. She hadn't yet won the fight raging inside her—the one that told her to give in to the physical temptation of becoming Luca's lover and to hell with the consequences. The problem was she knew that anything they started now would *not* end happily. She feared it'd end in heartbreak. *Her* heartbreak.

Her eyes stung. He really meant to sacrifice himself on that altar of duty. A woman like her—an interloper into his world with a nightmare of a family—had no hope of changing his mind.

What really broke her heart, though, was that he understood the sacrifice he was making. His white-lipped determination that Benny would never have to make the same sacrifice had told her that.

'Good evening, Signorina Thomas.'

She turned. 'Signor Romano! It's nice to see you again.'

'You are looking a little serious. I hope nothing is wrong?'

*Seriously?* He of all men could ask that? When he'd been a co-conspirator of this ridiculous plan to marry Luca off to the highest bidder? For a moment her throat closed over.

In the awkward pause that followed, he said, 'I hear you visited Gianni's earlier in the week.'

It was the perfect opening. And she couldn't resist. 'I enjoyed my visit very much. Luca told me of Gianni's history, his grandfather's distress that it had been sold off, as well as how he means to win it back—the plan you and his grandfather have concocted for him.'

'He told you all this?' Signor Romano's jowls worked before he thrust out his jaw. 'No doubt you subscribe to more modern views, as my daughter does, and disapprove?'

She needed to tread carefully *and* tactfully.

*Asset, remember, not a liability.*

But Luca had given her her heart's desire. If she could help him in return, she would.

'It's not my place to approve or disapprove, Signor Romano. As I am younger than you, however, it's perfectly true—and natural, I might add—for my views to be more modern than yours…like your daughter's.'

She met the older man's eyes squarely. 'I've told Luca that if he attempts to pressure Benny into marrying for duty rather than love, I'll intervene.'

'Pah! You all think the new-fangled ways are better, but they no more guarantee happiness than the old ways. My Bella fancies herself in love with a man I consider unsuitable. If she follows her heart, it will be broken.'

'And yet if she follows your bidding, you will break her heart instead.'

His head rocked back.

'Why is this young man unsuitable, Signor Romano? Because he's not from your social class?'

He didn't answer, but the set of his mouth told her that her guess was correct.

'Does he not have a job?'

He huffed and puffed for a moment but then shrugged. 'He has a perfectly good job in the city. From all accounts, he works hard.'

She shrugged too. 'So far so good. Does he have a good circle of friends? That's always a good reference for a man's character.'

Did Luca have many friends? He spoke warmly of his cousins. And yet one of them was betraying him.

'Yes, yes. He plays in a soccer team…keeps in touch with his school and university friends… takes part in work socials.'

From where she was standing, the man didn't

sound unsuitable at all. 'So the only strike against him,' she started slowly, 'is that he's not a billionaire?'

Both of them were silent for a long moment, staring out at the partygoers. 'You want the best for your daughter. You want to protect her from harm and hurt. I understand that. I'd do anything to protect my little Fern from harm.'

When she turned back, the indignation had faded from his eyes. 'You think I should meet her young man?'

'I can't see what harm it'd do.'

'It could get her hopes up.'

She smiled. 'I think you're worried you might like her young man.'

He harrumphed. 'Why do you care anyway? I think, perhaps, you want Luca for yourself.'

Her heart clenched, but she refused to allow his words to rile her. 'Luca's a very attractive man, he has a generous heart...and he's been very kind to me.' She pulled in a breath and made herself smile. 'But I'm not the woman for him. The choices he makes, though, will affect Benny.'

'And you are fond of your godson.'

She loved him. And the thought of leaving him and returning to Australia—

She shied away from the thought. 'I expect your Bella is every bit as honourable as Luca and would treat Benny well. And I know Luca would do just about anything to make his grandfather— and you—proud.'

'*Me?*'

She glanced up in surprise. 'He looks up to you in a way he wishes he could look up to his own father.'

'I...'

'I don't think giving Luca a wife he respects but doesn't love, a woman who will spend her whole life pining for another man, is the answer, Signor Romano. It's a recipe for misery. Misery that the two of them will do all they can to hide from you and his grandfather. But it will create a wedge between you all.'

Good Lord. She hadn't meant to say so much. It wasn't her place, but... 'If your worst fears are confirmed about Bella's beau and he does break her heart, at least she can be certain of your unconditional love and turn to you for comfort and support.'

He stilled. 'There is a ring of wisdom to your words.'

She tried to smile. 'All my life I've wished for a father who wanted to see me happy, as you do Bella.'

His eyes gentled. 'And this you do not have?'

'No.' She glanced across at the broad-shouldered figure across the room. 'Neither, I think, does Luca.'

'His grandfather loves him.'

She turned back to Signor Romano. 'Does he? Not above everything else. While you are primarily concerned with your daughter's happiness, Signor Vieri Senior is primarily concerned with regaining the jewel in his empire's crown. But who's primarily concerned with Luca's happiness?'

Signor Romano's mouth dropped open.

'It seems to me that Luca has to pay the price for his parents', aunts' and uncles' greed and recklessness, as well as his grandfather's mismanagement.'

'Monique!'

She swung to find Luca directly behind them—his eyes blazing and his face pinched white. Her heart thundered in her ears, but she refused to lower her chin. 'And I don't think that's fair,' she finished.

'You have no right to speak of this.'

He clenched his hands so hard his whole body shook. His voice, low and fierce, stung. She'd overstepped the mark. She'd known it all along, but she hadn't been able to stop.

She turned back to Signor Romano. 'Luca is right. I spoke out of turn. If I gave offence, I sincerely apologise.'

Signor Romano shook his head. 'She gave no offence, Luca. In fact, she gave an old man a new perspective.'

Luca blinked.

'Please, will you both excuse me?'

The older man left, and Monique tried not to wince as she glanced up at Luca. 'How angry are you?'

Some of the fire in his eyes died. 'I do not know. Signor Romano seemed almost pleased with your conversation.' He frowned. 'With you raking him over the coals.'

She pulled herself up to her full height, which was still woefully shy of Luca's six feet two inches. 'I did no such thing! He spoke to me about Bella, and I gave him my opinion. I think now he's going to at least meet the man she's in love with.'

'How…?' He shook himself. '*Why* would you do such a thing?'

'To get you off the hook.'

'Monique.' His voice held a note of warning.

'And because I don't want a rift to occur between father and daughter.' She glanced to where the older man was now in conversation with a group of people across the room. 'It must be lovely to have a father who cares for you so deeply.'

She started when Luca's warm hand closed about hers. 'Yes,' he agreed.

She squeezed his hand and sent him what she hoped was a buck-up smile. 'We'll do better. Benny and Fern will have at least one parent they can always rely on, who will always do their best for them. They'll know they're loved.'

His mouth firmed. 'I will do everything in my power to ensure my son's happiness.'

She believed him.

'Now…' he straightened '…you do not have a drink. Have you had ample to eat? Let me get you a glass of champagne and something sweet to nibble.'

'Are you hungry?' Luca said when they returned to the villa later that evening.

'How can I be hungry when you plied me with food all evening?' Ever since confessing she'd gone to bed hungry—that one single time— he'd brought titbits up to the nursery after dinner every night. She'd been treated to bowls of luscious raspberries, ripe peaches, and decadent mouth-watering pastries.

She wasn't hungry, but… 'I'm going to make a cup of tea. Would you like one?'

'You wish to speak to me about something?'

The man always cut to the heart of the matter. She nodded and he gestured for her to precede him into the kitchen.

'I hope Benito is giving you no cause for alarm?'

'None at all.' She put the kettle on and made tea, pushed a biscuit tin towards him. 'Fern and I made Anzac biscuits today—an Australian speciality. It'll make her day if you try one and tell her tomorrow how much you enjoyed it.'

He immediately reached into the tin, and bit into a biscuit. His eyes widened. '*Delizioso!* My new favourite. I will tell her so in the morning.'

Fern and Luca were developing the loveliest of friendships. She bit her lip. Friendship was fine, but...

Fern had suffered too much loss already in her short life. She couldn't allow her niece to start relying on Luca too much. It might be time to start talking to Fern about all the fun they'd have once they returned to Australia—start reconciling her to their future, a future that didn't include Italy or Luca.

She forced her chin up. It wasn't like they'd never see Luca and Benny again. There'd be visits and video calls. They'd simply become part of the wider landscape of each other's lives. Which was fine. Perfectly fine.

'What did you wish to speak to me about?'

She snapped back and glanced at him, hoping he'd take what she had to say in good part—in the way she meant it to be taken. 'Tonight I met several women who I expect are on the list of Suitable Prospective Brides.' She sipped her tea. 'How well do you know these women, Luca?'

His nostrils flared. 'You are again overstepping the mark.'

She couldn't tell if the words were a reprimand or not. It sounded as if he was simply stating a fact. He looked almost...resigned.

She winced an apology. 'I can't seem to help it.'

She could've sworn his lips twitched at her confession.

'It's just… The woman you marry will affect Benny.'

'You think I would choose a wife who would be unkind to him?'

'Not on purpose.' But men could be stupid when it came to women, and she worried that his drive to provide his grandfather with all that the older man wanted would blind him to other things. 'You knew Bella well, obviously, as you said you grew up together. But some of the women I met this evening are awfully young.'

His eyebrows shot up.

'For example, how well do you know Siena Bianchi?

'I've spent very little time one on one with her, but she has always been bright and personable. I have done business with her mother and was impressed with her. Do you have something negative to say about Siena?'

'Not at all. I had an absolutely delightful chat with her. She's friendly and fun—wanted to know all about Australia as she's hoping to travel there one day. She doesn't have a snobbish bone in her body.'

He straightened. 'This is an excellent reference.'

'Except for one minor detail.'

'And that is?'

'She likes women, not men.'

He stared at her blankly.

'She's gay, Luca.'

'How do you know this?'

She raised an eyebrow.

Siena had made a pass at Monique? Luca nearly swallowed his tongue. Did Monique prefer women to men too? He could've sworn...

'And you?' He couldn't prevent the question slipping from his lips.

She sent him the oddest look. 'I'm heterosexual.'

The pounding of his heart slowed. 'Good.'

Her brow knotted. 'Why good?'

*Dio!* What was he thinking?

'I didn't think you'd be so...' she edged away '...narrow-minded.'

'No! That is not what I meant. I...' He rolled his shoulders. 'I'm merely relieved my instincts haven't led me astray completely.'

A fraught, awkward silence slammed into place. He could've kick himself for causing it. For making them both aware of the attraction that simmered just under the surface whenever they were alone together. The attraction they were doing their best to ignore.

She moistened her lips. He would *not* notice

their shine or acknowledge the siren song they sang to him.

'You aren't going to rush into marriage, are you? You will take the time to get to know a woman well before you propose to her?'

'Of course.'

But the assurance sounded hollow. This hypothetical marriage had seemed an entirely different proposition when Bella had been his prospective bride. He and Bella were friends, he trusted her. He'd known what he was getting into. Now, though...

When Monique was in the room, he couldn't focus on any other woman, barely saw any other women!

He needed to put an end to this dating arrangement. The ground he and Monique were now treading...the lines had become too blurred. The way she'd spoken to Signor Romano this evening had proved that.

'You wish to select my bride for me?'

She choked on her tea. 'Absolutely not!'

'Then why are you vetting these women?'

'To show you what a crazy idea it is to make such a *practical* marriage.'

Exhaustion swept through him. He wanted to close his eyes and rest his head on his arms.

'Luca, don't you want to believe in a strong and true romantic love that will add happiness and strength to your life? It's what I hope and wish for. It's what most people hope and wish for.'

His heart burned. He couldn't afford such sentimentality.

He recalled her words to Signor Romano and his heart burned all the fiercer.

She glanced down at her hands. 'There are other kinds of love that are just as important, of course. Like the love one has for their child—like the love you have for Benny.'

'And you for Fern.'

She bit her lip, glancing away. 'Having Fern is all I've wanted for so long.'

For the first time it occurred to him that it had been unfair of him to ask her to come to Rome. She should've been free to build her life with Fern away from any complications he and his life could create for her.

But the wage he was paying her, and the freedom she had to now finish her childcare qualifications… Those things would help her provide Fern with security. That had to mean something, surely? And then there was her love for Benny. She'd wanted to help him settle into his new life. She'd needed to see him happy and safe.

'I don't need anything else. I don't want to want anything else.'

Her words hauled him back. 'But you deserve so much more.' She deserved to find the strong and lasting romantic love of which she dreamed.

She glanced up with wide eyes, swallowed and nodded. 'I think you deserve so much more too, Luca.'

*Who has Luca's best interests at heart?*

The pulse at the base of her jaw fluttered. He stared at it, his mouth going dry.

'I don't think anyone has the right to choose your wife for you. I think you should be free to make your own choice.'

'Why are you so set on changing my mind?' He could tell she thought it would add to his happiness, but why did she care? Because he'd given her her heart's desire and she felt she owed him?

She stared at his mouth for a long moment and then shook herself. 'Because you deserve to have someone on your side.'

This woman! Her lips tempted him, but her words undid him. He couldn't help it. His mouth swooped down to hers before common sense could kick back in. And the moment their lips touched common sense scattered on the four winds.

Her lips were warm and soft, spiced with the sweetness of the tea she'd been drinking, and utterly addictive. After the briefest of hesitations, when she'd bowed under the surprise of his initial onslaught, one of her hands slid around the back of his head to hold him close while she kissed him back with a fervour that made the blood stampede in his veins.

His knee knocked the table as he turned more directly towards her and his elbow too as he cradled her face in his hands and swept his tongue across her lips. Her free hand landed on his knee as if to brace against the barrage of sensations that assailed her as his tongue explored the softness of her mouth, enticing her tongue to dance in a kiss that threw every caution to the wind.

Her fingers curled into the firmness of his thigh muscle as if to hold him there, as if to prevent him from moving away. He wasn't going anywhere! But he needed more, needed to feel more of her.

Hauling them both to their feet, he pressed her close, moulding her curves against him—her softness to his hardness. His hand roved across her back and in response she plastered herself against him as if there was nowhere she'd rather be.

The taste of her…the feel of her in his arms… It was like nothing he'd ever experienced. This woman had found her way into his blood, was now imprinted there, never to be forgotten and always to be craved. Throwing back his head, he sucked in a breath. Her hands moved from around his waist to explore the planes of his chest and shoulders through the cotton of his shirt. Her touch sparked explosions of sensation across his skin.

Dazed eyes met his again and her kiss-swollen lips were an invitation he couldn't resist. His head dipped and she met him halfway in a kiss that tasted like sunshine and joy, wrapped inside a fierceness to rival a summer storm.

Pressing his lips along the line of her throat, he concentrated on her sighs and the tiny sounds she made in the back of her throat, greedy for more, greedy to hear his name on her lips. He cupped one of her sweet, lush breasts through the thin material of her dress, the nipple hardening against his palm. Her gasp dived straight to his groin.

He needed this woman. He needed her naked and writhing beneath him. Every instinct he had told him he would find heaven in her arms, and he craved that with every fibre of himself. But he could not take her on the kitchen table where anyone could walk in!

Holding tight to her upper arms, he held her away from him a fraction so she could meet his gaze.

'What are you saying?' she whispered.

Only then did he realise that he was murmuring in his native tongue. 'That you are bewitching, magnificent…beautiful. That I want you.'

He stared into those amber eyes. 'You make me feel things I never have before. Please, spend the night with me, *tesoro*. Let me make love to you. Let me—'

Soft fingers pressed to his lips halted his flow of words.

She dragged in a breath that made her entire body tremble. 'You make me feel too much.'

'I want the chance to make you feel even more, *cara*.'

She stared, her chest heaving. 'You're suggesting we have a fling? Like the one you and Anita had?'

Her brow furrowed as she mentioned Anita's name, and ice trickled through him. This was no way to win back the respect and reverence for the Vieri name that his grandfather so craved. He no longer had the luxury of acting the playboy.

It was as if she could see that thought flash through his eyes, because she huffed out a laugh. 'Have you given a moment's thought about what would be said if anyone found out we were having an affair? You know my family is utterly disreputable—the papers would say you were consorting with drug addicts and criminals.'

'I know *you* are not like that, Monique.'

'It doesn't change the fact that you wouldn't want to be associated with a family like mine for even a single moment.'

She stepped away, placing her hands on the back of her chair as if she needed its support. 'Before Fern came to live with me the first time, I had a sort of boyfriend.'

Jealousy pooled hot and dark in his gut. '*Sort of* boyfriend?'

'A friends with benefits type of arrangement.'

Dear God. If she suggested such an arrangement for them… 'What happened?' he asked, grinding his back molars together.

'When Fern came to live with me, he stopped coming around, and he stopped calling.'

The fool!

'And I realised that the friendship part of our relationship had meant nothing at all to him.'

The expression in her eyes made him want to tear this unknown man from limb to limb.

'While I'd considered the friendship the most important part of all.' She glanced up, her eyes unfamiliarly dark. 'I made a vow to myself then that I'd never get involved with an emotionally unavailable man again.' She pressed her hands to her stomach. 'And, Luca, you're about as emotionally unavailable as they come.'

He wanted to protest against this conclusion. But… 'You are right. I am sorry. Please forgive my lack of control this evening.'

'We both lost control.' She dragged in a breath. 'We just have to do better in the future.'

He made a decision then and there. 'It is time to end this plus one arrangement.'

She hesitated, but then nodded.

He thought hard, came to a decision quickly. 'It will be best if I leave Rome for a few weeks.' If he was no longer in the city, his inability to attend certain events might be overlooked. But even if it wasn't, even if he did cause grave offence in several quarters, it was time to prioritise. He needed to uncover the traitor within the company. There was little point in attempting to win respect through networking when he was being undermined at the grassroots.

And with all the recent changes in his life, it was too soon to be thinking of a wife. That needed to be put on hold until he had everything else sorted first.

'Please pack all that Benito, you and Fern will need for a few weeks. We'll leave on Monday.'

'Where are we going?'

'To my place in Tuscany.'

She nodded but didn't smile. 'I'll make sure we're ready.'

And then she was gone.

He dropped back into his chair and rested his head in his hands. A man of honour would not go after her. A man of honour would stop thinking of her in any other way except as his child's godmother. A man of honour would concentrate on earning back his family's good name and assuring his peers that he was a man who could be trusted.

None of that could rid his body's hunger for her. *Enough!* There was too much at stake to risk it on a brief affair. Benny needed Monique. His relationship with his godmother was too important to endanger. And Luca was determined to do better by his child than his parents had done by him.

He pushed back his shoulders. He would do what his grandfather had always done. He'd act honourably.

# CHAPTER EIGHT

MONIQUE STARED OUT of the car window at rolling green hills, rambling vineyards and stone farmhouses and told herself to focus and take it all in. This was a once-in-a-lifetime trip. Who knew if she'd ever see this part of the world again? She should be storing it up so she could tell everyone at home about it.

But all she could focus on was the unnatural quiet that stretched through the car.

Luca had told her it'd take roughly three and a half hours to reach his *'little place in Tuscany'*. He'd told her it was a converted farmhouse on a little land. He'd even volunteered the information that a woman came up from the nearby village every day to cook and clean whenever Luca stayed.

*That* had been the extent of their conversation. Sparkling, right? And with the children dozing on the back seat, the quiet that had descended on the car was anything but comfortable.

She considered instigating conversation but dismissed that immediately. Luca was her boss.

*Boss. Boss. Boss.*

She tried to stamp that word on her brain. It wasn't her place to chatter away like a darned chipmunk. It'd only annoy him and wear her out. Lose-lose. If he wanted conversation, he could initiate it.

She bit back a sigh. If only he acted like her boss and treated her like the hired help. If only she *felt* like the hired help.

Dragging her phone from her handbag, she snapped a couple of happy snaps of the countryside to at least give the impression she was appreciating it...and not obsessing over that stupid kiss.

He glanced at her, but even before she could consider turning to meet those dark eyes, his gaze had returned to the front again, his attention shifting back to driving, capable hands relaxed on the wheel. She forced her hands to stop gripping her phone so hard. 'It's beautiful countryside.'

'*Sì.*'

*Smile.*

She folded her hands and gritted her teeth. What the hell had she been about, kissing this man?

*He kissed you first. He took you off guard. He—*

As if that made any difference! She hadn't discouraged him. She'd kissed him back with an eagerness that should make her blush. It didn't. It

simply had heat rising through her in a tidal wave
of want again.

She shifted on her seat. Luca's knuckles whit-
ened on the steering wheel and a pulse thudded
in her throat. Could he sense her need...her frus-
tration? Did he share it?

*Stop it!*

She did what she could to unclench her thighs
and slow her breathing.

A quick glance informed her that his knuckles remained white so she shifted her gaze from
the front windscreen to the side passenger window, where she could spare herself the temptation of surveying him in her peripheral vision.
She needed to wrangle her wayward desires back
under control and remind herself of all the reasons kissing him was the worst idea in the history of the world.

Top of that list, of course, was Fern and Benny.
She couldn't let anything that happened between
her and Luca affect them. That would be unfor-
givable.

She wanted, needed—had promised Anita—
to create a lifelong relationship with Benny. She
took the role of godmother seriously. She knew
the impact one person could have on a life, and
she meant to have a good and lasting impact on
Benny's. She couldn't do anything that would
risk jeopardising that. If things between her and
Luca became...messy, if she somehow alienated

Luca, there'd be no denying it would impact on her and her godson's relationship. She owed it to Benny, and she owed it to Anita, to prevent that from happening.

She owed Fern her full focus too. Her niece didn't deserve a mother figure who was mooning over some man. Fern needed Monique to be fully engaged in their future life together—to show her how to be happy and trust in their future. Not worrying because she sensed her aunt's unhappiness and discontent.

Not that she *was* unhappy or discontented.

Besides, she deserved better too. Luca had given her so much—he'd rescued Fern, he'd given her this opportunity to strengthen her bond with Benny—and she couldn't help feeling she'd let him down in their plus one arrangement, but there was only so far gratitude could and should extend, and she refused to be a martyr to it.

She also refused to pretend that she thought his plan to marry for practical business reasons a good idea. It had disaster written all over it. As his friend she couldn't pretend it was anything else. Not that he'd ever agree with her. And it wasn't like she was actually his friend either, was she?

A fling with her wouldn't change his mind. And although she knew she wasn't the kind of woman he'd ever consider marrying—could her family be any more opposite to his requirements?—if they became intimate…if they had a fling…

A forbidden thrill raced up her spine. Beneath the security of her bra, her breasts grew heavy and her nipples beaded. She gritted her teeth and concentrated on her breathing.

If she and Luca had a fling, and he still went ahead with his cold and clinical marriage, she'd take it as a personal affront. Even though she had no expectation of him becoming serious about her.

It didn't make any sense!

The one thing she did know was that a fling with Luca would complicate everything.

And neither of them needed the drama and inconvenience of that kind of complication at this point in their lives.

'See that farmhouse on the hill?'

She glanced to where Luca pointed; glad to give her mind something new to focus on.

'That is our destination—Casa Speranza.'

Casa Speranza. She repeated it in her mind, fixing it there so she could look up what it meant later.

'It is my home away from home.'

Just for a moment his face cleared, and her chest clenched in response. Whatever else Casa Speranza might mean, it was clear he loved this place.

From here the farmhouse looked large, but it wasn't the huge castle she'd half expected. Grapevines swept down the hillside and through the surrounding fields, and everything looked rich and lush and full of promise. A sigh eased out of her. It *looked* like a home.

'Do you own the vineyard as well?'

He nodded. 'We grow Trebbiano grapes—a white variety we sell to a local distillery famed for its brandy.'

A snippet from a previous conversation came back to her. 'Is this where your grandfather lives?'

'His holding is ninety minutes further north, but he is away from home at the moment, cruising the Mediterranean as the guest on a dear friend's yacht.'

She shook her head. What a life.

'She gestured at the hill. 'How big is it?'

'Thirty acres. It is only small.'

It didn't sound small to her!

Ten minutes later she walked through the front door into a stone-flagged room with beamed ceilings. 'It's lovely!' It was cool and shady and incredibly welcoming, and as she stood there the tension started to slip away.

'If I could, I would spend all of my time here.'

His shoulders had lost some of their hard edges too. 'Then maybe you ought to arrange it so you can.' His entire demeanour told her how much happier he'd be here than in Rome.

'You have an over-inflated sense of the extent of my freedom, Monique.'

She glanced up and their gazes caught and clashed. 'I've seen your home office in Rome,

Luca. I don't see why you couldn't establish a similar one here. Just because your parents, aunts and uncles were such hedonists, it doesn't mean you have to be their polar opposite. You're allowed enjoyment and ease too. You're allowed happiness.'

It wasn't her place to say such things! 'Of course,' she managed to choke out, 'what will make you happy is entirely up to you to decide.'

*And don't you forget it.*

Wordlessly he led her through to the back of the house to a large modern kitchen with a huge open-plan dining and living space. French doors led out to a paved courtyard with a view that stretched over gold and green hills and fields. In the distance a stand of cypress trees stood dark olive against a blue sky and a river sparkled silver as it meandered through the valley.

She clasped her hands beneath her chin and gobbled it all up with a greed she didn't bother trying to hide. 'It's extraordinarily beautiful. And so peaceful. No wonder you love it so much.'

'More beautiful than Mirror Glass Bay?'

She momentarily froze. Why would he ask her such a thing? 'Different,' she managed, her voice unaccountably husky.

'Come,' he said, all brusqueness again. 'I will show you the rest of the house. The children will wake soon.' They'd set the sleeping children on the sofas in the front room.

There was a downstairs bathroom and laundry room, as well as a formal dining room. He gestured to the right of the front door. 'That is my study.' And upstairs there were four generous bedrooms—one a master with an en suite bathroom—as well as a large family bathroom.

She chose the bedroom furthest from the master for herself.

'I think you'll find we'll all be comfortable,' he said.

He was careful not to meet her eyes. She was careful not to meet his. 'More than comfortable,' she agreed, following him back down the stairs. She'd injected a cheerfulness she was far from feeling into her voice and the words rang out too bright and shiny. Behind his back, she grimaced. For heaven's sake, get a grip.

He swung around when they reached the bottom of the stairs and she did all she could to smooth out her face.

'I assume I can leave you to settle the children and organise their lunch?'

'Of course.'

'I'll bring in the suitcases and then must get to work.' He gestured to the door of his study.

'So this is a working holiday, then?' she called out before he disappeared through the front door.

He turned back, his magnificent physique backlit by the sun. The sight pulled her skin tight across her bones with an ache impossible to ignore. His face, though, was in shade, making it impossible to see his expression.

'This is not a holiday, Monique.'

It wasn't?

'It was merely imperative I leave Rome. It is as simple as that.' And then he was gone.

Released from the intensity of his presence, she slumped. Imperative he leave Rome? Because she'd failed as his plus one? An entirely different burn took up residence in her chest then.

After taking the suitcases upstairs, Luca retreated to his study. Closing the door behind him, he rested his back against it and closed his eyes.

*Dio.* He had to get the better of this *spell* that had him in its grip. He couldn't look at Monique without wanting to drag her into his arms and kiss her until neither one of them could think straight. He continued to relive those few short moments that she'd spent in his arms on Saturday night, aching to repeat them.

He'd found heaven.

But that particular brand of heaven was not meant for him. Striding over to his desk, he switched on his computer and forced himself into his chair. A moment later he was on his feet again, pacing, eventually halting by the window to glare at the terraced landscape outside with its rows of grapevines marching down the hill.

He'd come here to find peace. For as long as

Monique remained in residence, though, he'd find none of that.

*Send her back to Rome.*

The thought whispered through him, the instant remedy tempting him.

A moment later he slashed a hand through the air. She was Benito's nanny, his *godmother*. He couldn't treat her with such casual disregard simply because he found her presence unsettling.

*Benito's godmother.*

That thought should bolster his resolve and give him strength. Monique was Benito's godmother—a relationship too important for him to risk in the pursuit of a temporary affair. He would control this hunger in his blood, this craving. He was a civilised man, for God's sake, not a beast.

Besides, while Monique might find him attractive, she'd indicated zero interest in any kind of temporary relationship of an intimate nature. She'd walked away from him on Saturday night with considerable—and enviable—ease.

She was fiercely independent, and she wanted to build a good future for her niece in Australia. He had no business, no right whatsoever, distracting her from such a noble goal. No, he would leave her in peace. He would prove to himself and the world that he was better than his parents.

He spent the afternoon shut in his study. He only emerged to feed Benito his dinner and get him ready for bed. He then took his own dinner into his study and shut the door firmly behind him.

Like a coward.

*Not* a coward—a sensible man. The less time he spent alone with the delectable Monique, the less likely his resolve was to falter. Besides, she had her studies to occupy her and she didn't need his presence interrupting her.

Eventually, though, he could no longer concentrate on his computer screen, the four walls of the room closing in on him. Emerging into the living room, he collapsed full-length onto a sofa, resting his head back against the soft cushioning, and tried to will the peace he always found here at Casa Speranza into his soul.

*Breathe in for the count of four. Hold for the count of four. Breathe out on the count of four. Hold. Repeat. Again. And again.*

Very slowly the tightness in his neck and shoulders began to ease and he found he could draw air deeper into his lungs. It felt like an age since he'd been able to breathe so freely and deeply. When was the last time he'd been for a run? Cardio exercise was good for increasing lung capacity. Tomorrow he would wake early and—

'Casa Speranza... Casa Speranza... *Casa* means home...'

His eyes sprang open at the softly murmured words. Monique. Staring intently at her phone.

He feasted his eyes on her. He couldn't help

it. How could she look so fresh and vibrant after that long car journey *and* having kept two demanding children happily occupied for most of the day on her own?

She wore the softest of thin lounge pants that did nothing to hide her beguiling shape and a T-shirt of sky-blue that highlighted the blonde highlights in her caramel hair. Yearning rose through him, swift and fast, piercing every defence he'd been at such pains to erect for the past two days.

'*Speranza...speranza...*' she murmured, still staring at her phone. 'It means...'

'Hope,' they both said at the same time.

She nearly dropped her phone as Luca sat up and placed his feet on the floor. 'I... I didn't notice you there. I—'

She broke off to study him through narrowed eyes. 'You look pale...and awfully tired.' Her frown deepened. 'Are you coming down with something?'

He shook his head. 'I am merely weary from too much work and not enough exercise and fresh air. I have not been sleeping well.' His sleep had been disturbed by dreams of a golden woman beckoning to him, but somehow remaining out of reach, no matter how hard he tried to catch up to her. 'I will go for a run tomorrow and that will set me to rights again.'

An awkward silence ensued.

'Casa Speranza.' She moistened her lips. 'Home of Hope. It's a beautiful name for a beautiful place.'

Her approbation warmed him all the way through. 'I am glad you approve.'

'Well…' she sent him a tight smile, edging towards the stairs '… I'll leave you to enjoy the peace.'

It took all his strength to resist the impulse to ask her to stay. A sudden thought, though, made him stiffen. 'Monique?'

She turned at the foot of the stairs, one hand on the banister.

'You are not worried that…' His throat clenched and he had to clear it before he could continue speaking. 'That I will force my attentions onto you? If you are, allow me to assure you—'

'No!' Her eyes widened and she took a step towards him, before halting and pressing a hand to her abdomen. 'Of course I'm not. You're a man of honour. You'd never—'

She closed her eyes and dragged in a deep breath, before meeting his gaze. 'No, Luca, I am not afraid of that. Not at all.'

He fought a frown. Did that mean she was afraid of something else?

'I merely plan to have an early night. I've not been sleeping well either.'

The pleating of her brow and the pursing of her lips told him she wished she'd not confessed as much. Had she not been sleeping for the same reasons as him? The dragon he'd been doing his best to lull lifted its head.

Her swift intake of breath and the way her eyes flared in answer to whatever she saw in his face told him she recognised his hunger, and that she shared it. His every atom came to electrified life.

She swung away from him and raced up the stairs, her 'Goodnight' drifting down to him like a taunt.

Dropping his head to his hands, he cursed fluently and swiftly in three different languages. Tomorrow he would punish his body with such a gruelling run it would dull and exhaust all these wayward impulses and help to cleanse him of this inconvenient attraction.

By the time he returned from his run the next morning, Luca ached all over. Monique was already in the kitchen with the children, feeding them their breakfast. He stopped to talk to the children and eat a slice of toast he barely tasted. He and Monique barely exchanged half a dozen words.

He locked himself in his study for the rest of the day. At one point, the children's laughter drew him to the window. He watched them romp and play with Monique, all of them laughing in the warm sunshine. An entirely different yearning rose through him then. This was the childhood he'd wanted for himself. It was exactly what he

wanted for Benito—warmth, security, laughter…
love. As he watched his son drag himself to a
standing position, holding onto Monique's hands,
at the way he smiled up into his godmother's face,
he saw how much Benito loved her.

*Dio.* How would he ever replace her?

A daring thought burrowed under his skin and
started to chafe him. Maybe he didn't have to replace her? Maybe she'd consider staying as *her
Benny's* nanny forever? He rubbed a hand across
his jaw. Would she give up her dream of running
her own childcare centre for that?

With an oath, he swung away from the window.
He suspected the answer would be, 'No'.

Still, there was no denying she loved Benito.
She'd sacrifice much to ensure his happiness and
security. And yet what kind of man would ask her
to make such a sacrifice?

A humourless laugh sounded through him. Besides, how would he ever settle on a wife if Monique remained? He didn't notice other women
whenever she was near.

He found no answer to the questions that continued to plague him. He wanted nothing more
than to cast them aside and join the happy trio
outside for a few short hours and leave the future
to fend for itself.

*In the same way your parents lived their lives?
Like your aunts and uncles?*

He clenched his hands so hard his entire frame started to shake. No, he was better than that.

When a ping sounded from his computer to announce an incoming email, he obeyed the summons and forced himself back behind his desk. He needed to focus on what he owed the Vieri Corporation—his grandfather, cousins and the generations that were to follow. He would uncover the defector within their midst and cut out the corrupt heart that continued to beat within the company. Once that was done, maybe then he could reassess his future.

A half-formed hope he barely dared acknowledge had started to form inside him. If he could safeguard the Vieri Corporation's future, strengthen its very foundations, and make those foundations virtually unassailable... Wouldn't that be enough? Wouldn't a dynastic marriage then be unnecessary?

If he did everything else right, maybe he could reconcile his grandfather to a new way of moving the company forward. The thought of disappointing his grandfather, the man who had given him so much, sent a bruise blooming over his soul. However, his grandfather wasn't an unreasonable man and if Bella's father could be brought to see a different path for his daughter, then it didn't seem so impossible that his grandfather could be brought to see a different future for Luca too.

Maybe.

* * *

When Luca emerged from his study later that evening, he found Monique curled up on one of the sofas, a mug of tea—he sniffed the air, peppermint—on the coffee table, its steam curling into the air. Her eyes raced over the page of the book she held. She turned the page with eager zeal, read the last few lines of the chapter and then let the book drop to her lap.

Only then did she glance up at him, her mouth forming a perfect O. 'Now, I didn't see that coming! The plot thickens.' She held the cover up so he could see—an old Agatha Christie paperback. 'The bookcase is full of them, and I can't believe I've never read her before. This is brilliant.'

He eased down into the sofa opposite and took note of the title, making a resolution to read it once she'd finished. 'I can't remember the last time I read a book.'

'Because you work too hard.' She shook her head, setting her book on the coffee table and reaching for her mug. 'Knowing all you want to achieve, I'm gobsmacked—completely and utterly gobsmacked—that you—'

She broke off, going bright red.

He stared. What had she been about to say? 'That I... What?'

She wrinkled her nose. 'It was nothing...an utter impertinence. Forget it.'

Now he was really intrigued. 'Tell me.' He kept his voice gentle. 'I promise I will not be angry.'

'Even though it's none of my business *and* far too personal?'

He found himself laughing. 'Why does this not surprise me?'

The smile she sent him was rueful, and then she stared at him as if he utterly baffled her. 'It's just… Luca, I know how driven you are, and I applaud your goal to re-establish the Vieri family's good name.'

'But?'

'No buts, just… How on earth did you find the time to not only have a holiday but a holiday fling while you were at it?' she said in a rush. 'It seems so out of character.'

The weariness he'd been fighting all day beat at him again now.

'See?' she said when he remained silent. 'I told you it was none of my business. You don't have to answer.'

'A week before I took that *impromptu* holiday…'

Her gaze sharpened at his emphasis.

'My grandfather came to me with his plan for Bella and I to marry. Or if I didn't think Bella and I would suit explained why another similarly suitable marriage would not only augment our cause but expedite it.'

She stared at him with troubled eyes.

'That holiday was my last hurrah before I buckled down to duty and responsibility.'

Her face softened. 'Your final rebellion. A farewell to youth and fun.'

'Not fun.' He refused to believe his life would be devoid of pleasure, regardless of what path he took. 'But a farewell to the single life, yes.' He lifted a shoulder in what felt like an altogether inadequate shrug. 'And Anita made me laugh, she was excellent company, and she wanted to live in the moment.'

Monique nodded as if she agreed with everything he said.

'We had no thought that there'd be any consequences to our time together.'

'Yes, her pregnancy was a shock to her.'

He hesitated. 'We have not really spoken about her.'

She glanced at him, biting her lip. 'I didn't want to mention her in case it upset you.'

'While I have not mentioned her for fear your grief is still too raw.'

Her smile, brief but kind, made something inside of him tick harder and faster. 'Listen to us dancing around each other's feelings.'

A moment later he felt as if he'd been skewered on the end of a spear when her eyes pinned him to the spot.

'You had your fling...you said your goodbyes...

you let her go. And yet, despite what you promised your grandfather, you'd have offered to marry her.'

It was old-fashioned, he knew, but, yes. He would have offered Anita marriage.

'Which tells me there are things that matter more to you than making an advantageous marriage.'

It would've been the antithesis of honour to abandon the mother of his child.

'Can you imagine yourself married to Anita now, Luca?'

He did his best to remember the dark-haired, dark-eyed woman who had made him laugh and momentarily forget the weight he carried on his shoulders, but he could recall nothing of depth, nothing that carried weight. Which was why it was so important Benito had Monique in his life. Through her he would get the opportunity to know his mother.

'The truth?' he asked. 'Even if it sounds hard and unfeeling? Even though I don't want it to?'

'I don't want pretty lies, Luca.'

'You once told me I didn't know Anita, and that is true. We did not share our worries or concerns with each other, or our hopes and dreams. I do not know what she wanted out of life. All I know is that she liked mojitos, loved to dance, and was friendly to everyone.'

He stared at his hands. 'But, no, I cannot imagine myself married to her.'

# CHAPTER NINE

THE RUSH OF relief that raced through her had Monique closing her eyes. She ought to feel appalled…and perhaps it was disloyal to Anita that she didn't. After all, Luca had been her best friend's lover and was the father of her child.

She did what she could to make sense of the thoughts whirling through her, desperately wanting to make peace with them. She'd loved Anita like a sister, missed her every single day. If she could change what had happened—the car accident that had taken her friend's life—she would in a heartbeat.

Dragging in a breath, she tried to imagine what Anita would say to her now if she were here.

Her friend hadn't been in love with Luca. She'd spoken of him fondly, but she hadn't pined for him, she hadn't turned every conversation round to him, she hadn't shed any tears, moped or sighed over him. In fact, after she'd told Monique about the fling and how much fun she'd had on her holiday, she hadn't mention him again until she'd discovered she was pregnant.

No, if anything were ever to happen between Luca and Monique, Anita wouldn't begrudge her friend that.

Not that anything *was* going to happen. But the knowledge made her breathe more easily all the same.

So did the knowledge that Luca wasn't nursing some secret unrequited love in his heart for her friend. She didn't want his attraction to her to be some kind of sticking plaster or panacea.

He'd admitted he barely knew Anita, but…

*Oh!*

She saw then what he wanted to know. How had she not realised sooner?

Pulling her phone from her pocket, she opened a folder on her photo app and came to sit beside him. His warmth and scent filled her senses, making every cell come alive, but she ignored it as best she could to angle her phone towards him. 'This is Anita, six months pregnant. You can see how well she looks…and how happy she is.'

He leaned in closer. 'Her smile, it could not be any wider!'

He reached out a finger as if to touch Anita's tummy. 'Was she this well throughout her pregnancy?'

'She had a couple of weeks of minor morning sickness in the early days, but after that she glowed. As soon as she found out she was having Benny she gave up coffee and alcohol. Not that she drank that much of either anyway. She did everything she could to make sure he'd be born healthy and happy.'

She showed him multiple photos of Anita as she'd progressed through her pregnancy, and then moved on to the photos of Benny as a newborn. 'I was Anita's birth partner.'

His jaw dropped. 'You were?'

She could only imagine how much she wished he'd been there, so she took her time describing the experience in as much detail as possible. 'It was the most amazing thing I've ever experienced. It felt like a miracle that at the end of it was this most incredibly perfect baby, with Anita counting all of his fingers and toes and radiating so much love that I cried.'

He handed her his handkerchief, and she realised her cheeks were wet with tears again now. She dried them, and then showed him the pictures she'd taken of Benny during the first seven months of his life. Some of them were of Benny on his own; others were with Anita, Anita's parents or with Monique. She told him the little stories that went along with each series of photographs. It was a joy to talk of that time, to talk about Anita and remember her with such clarity and affection.

'I have seen some of these photos, or others

like them. They were on Anita's computer and I have saved them for Benito, but you have given me the context.'

She met his gaze and suddenly realised how closely they'd drifted towards one another.

'You have given me such a gift. You make me feel almost as if I were there and a part of it.'

He should have been there. He *should* have been a part of it.

'I don't know how to thank you.'

'Not necessary.' Their shoulders touched, their thighs touched, and his mouth was too darned close. She should inch back, but she didn't.

'You miss her.'

He said it at the same time as she said, 'Did you ever find out who intercepted Anita's messages to you?'

They were both silent for two beats. 'Yes,' she said in answer to his question. 'I miss Anita every single day.'

'No,' he said in answer to hers. 'There does not seem to be any point now.' He stared at her. 'I'm sorry you lost your friend, Monique. I wish there was something I could do.'

'Thank you.'

'I didn't realise how close the two of you were.' He hesitated. 'Why were you not looking after Benny when I arrived from Italy?'

A pain, swift and sharp, pierced through the centre of her. 'Skye and my mother had gone to

Brisbane and left Fern with a neighbour. They were only supposed to be gone for a day. When they didn't return that evening the neighbour called me.' All the neighbours had Monique's contact details. 'They were gone for a week. I was afraid of the legal implications if I took Fern home to Mirror Glass Bay, so I stayed there to look after her. It was on my second day there that news of Anita's accident reached me.'

A truck driver had fallen asleep at the wheel and crossed several lanes of traffic to slam head on into the car Anita and her parents had been travelling in. They had been returning from a trip to see her mother's heart specialist. They'd been killed instantly. The truck driver was now facing manslaughter charges. Nothing good had come from the tragedy.

His hand closed about hers. 'I'm sorry.'

She shook herself. 'By the time I returned, Benny was already settled in the care of the local nurse-cum-social worker. She was another friend of mine and Anita's, and as she was staying next door with him and I could pop in whenever I liked...' And as they hadn't known if or when Monique might be called to Fern's aid again, it'd seemed like the best solution.

He nodded. 'I see.'

'That day at the motel when we first met, I'd come to your room to introduce myself and arrange a meeting with you to talk about Benny.'

'I am glad you appeared when you did. I knew Benito had a godmother and I had been meaning to contact you, but...'

'You were overwhelmed and still in shock.' He'd come a long way since that day. He and Benny had formed a loving relationship since then. Benny adored his father.

And if she wasn't careful she'd find herself equally smitten.

It took every ounce of strength she had, but she forced herself to her feet. 'It's getting late. It's time for me to say goodnight.'

The downward tilt of his lips, the way he went to speak and then stopped told her he wanted her to stay.

'Goodnight, Monique,' he said instead, and she fled.

'Did you finish your book?'

Luca strode into the living room the following evening and one look at him set her pulse galloping. She told herself she hadn't been sitting here, pretending to read and waiting for him to appear.

She suspected she might be a liar.

'It was fabulous. I've started another.' She held her current book up to show him.

'Excellent. Then I shall now read it.'

He was going to take the time to read a book? She schooled her features to hide her shock.

'You are surprised.'

The amused twist of his lips did the most dangerous things to her blood pressure. 'I'm merely glad to see you taking some R&R.'

'I have been taking stock of many things while we've been here.'

Just as he had yesterday evening, he sat on the sofa opposite. He wore low-slung jeans and the softest of dove-grey T-shirts that contrasted with his dark hair and olive skin. A bone-deep yearning stretched through her.

'Oh?' was all she could manage.

Instead of easing back against the sofa and relaxing into its softness, he planted his elbows on his knees and steepled his fingers. 'I have told you that someone in the Vieri Corporation—one of my cousins—is attempting to undermine all my grandfather and I are trying to achieve?'

She nodded.

'I am working hard to uncover the identity of this person or persons. It is why I am here, rather than in Rome. It is more important that I unmask this villain than pay court to my business associates in an attempt to ingratiate myself to them.'

'Are you getting close to discovering the guilty party?'

'Closer.' Those steepled fingers tapped twice against his mouth. 'We are hoping my being here will lull them into a false sense of security.'

'We?'

'My cousin Rosetta and I.'

She digested that piece of information. 'I see.'

'I'm not sure you do.' His gaze sharpened. 'Some of the things you have said to me over the past few weeks have made me stop to reassess what I want to achieve...and how I want to achieve it.'

*Her?*

'It is more important I discover who is causing this trouble within the company than continue the hunt for a wife my grandfather considers suitable.'

She agreed with that one hundred per cent.

'And do you know why?'

'Why?'

'Because it's the honourable thing to do.'

She couldn't stop her eyes from widening. Had he given up the idea of that marriage plan completely?

'Surely it is only right that I have the company's affairs in order before I ask a woman to share my life. My fate is tied to the company and, therefore, hers will be as well.'

'Absolutely. You wouldn't want to be accused of misleading anyone—especially not your future wife.'

'Exactly!'

He frowned. She bit the inside of her lip. 'Something's bothering you.'

He glanced up. 'I cannot help thinking that if Rosetta and I succeed at rooting out the deviant element within the company...'

Yes?'

'And then work hard to consolidate our position, surely that is proof enough of our intent to the wider world? After all, would we not be proclaiming by our very actions that our intentions are above board and honourable? And not just that, but that we also have the strength to withstand any internal leadership challenges.'

Her heart suddenly beat too hard and it was an effort to keep her voice steady. 'It makes sense to me.'

'Rosetta is extremely competent, and the company matters as much to her as it does to me. I've started to wonder why, when she's eighteen months my senior, my grandfather didn't make her CEO instead of me.' His eyes grew troubled. 'I begin to suspect the only reason I am CEO is because I am male.'

She could see the idea disturbed him.

'That is not fair, neither is it honourable. When the traitor in our ranks has been found and dealt with, Rosetta and I are going to restructure the current leadership model and become joint CEOs.'

She couldn't stop from clapping her hands. 'What a perfect solution!'

He smiled, true amusement lighting his eyes as he finally collapsed back against the sofa. 'I knew you would approve. It means that, in sharing the role, I will be at liberty to spend more time with Benito.'

'Both you and Rosetta will have the opportunity to have a family life alongside your careers. I think that's wonderful, Luca.'

A shadow crossed his face. 'My grandfather comes from an earlier generation when things were done differently. If he were to object to Rosetta's appointment as CEO, I would disagree with him. If he were to demand Rosetta make a marriage to shore up the Vieri name, I would fight against that.'

Everything inside her stilled. 'Are you saying what I think you're saying?'

He leaned forward again. 'What do you think I'm saying?'

She leaned forward too. 'That you recognise the hypocrisy of asking such a thing of yourself.'

Dark eyes throbbed into hers.

'That you're rethinking this plan to make a cold, business-like marriage because you recognise the cost is too high…and that ultimately it's unnecessary.'

'Si…' The word was drawn from his slowly. 'I must, of course, discuss all this with my grandfather at his earliest convenience. My cousins and I owe him everything. He worked hard and expanded the Vieri Corporation until it become one of the most successful entities in the world, and yet he taught us what it means to be a family too. Without his influence…' He broke off and shook his head. 'I don't like to think of what kind of man I'd be today if it wasn't for him. I might be as grasping and selfish as my parents.'

She doubted that. His grandfather had given him and his cousins not just an amazing financial legacy but something even more important—love. Like Signor Romano, though, the older man would be set in his ways. Still…

'He loves you, Luca, and he knows you love him. When you explain how you feel, he'll understand. Just as Signor Romano did with Bella.'

'I hope you're right.'

'You say he taught you the value of family. If that's the case I don't think you have anything to fear.' He and Signor Romano were good friends. They shared the same values and outlook. Once Luca had a chance to talk to his grandfather all would be well.

'Your words are wise and they give me hope.'

His smile, brief and dazzling, momentarily blinded her. She swallowed and forced her mind back to the conversation. 'If you can discover which of your cousins is double crossing you, surely that will prove your worth to your grandfather.' She hesitated before giving voice to a growing conviction. 'I think you ought to trace who intercepted the messages Anita sent to you, Luca. It might lead you to the traitor you're looking for.'

One eyebrow lifted. 'You are most anxious I discover that culprit.'

'It was a wicked thing they did.' They'd stolen seven months of his son's life from him. She'd loved every moment she'd spent with Benny, had loved being Anita's birth partner, but she didn't want any of that at the expense of the man in front of her. He should've had those experiences, not her.

'Then I will see what I can find out.'

He thought it was his parents. Instinct told her he also thought his parents were in league with this rogue cousin. That was why he was so suspicious that day he'd found his mother in his office. Maybe the one would lead to the other.

In the meantime, she wanted to rid him of the bitterness stretching through his eyes. 'I'm glad you're fighting for the life you deserve, Luca, and the marriage you deserve.'

She knew it made no difference to him and her. Their lives were too different, too incompatible. They had no future together. She knew that, but... 'You're a good man. You deserve to be happy.'

Her warmth and sincerity should have sent a corresponding warmth spreading through him. And it did. But it also unleashed a fierce heat into his blood. The heat didn't race through him like a bolt of lightning, but its inexorable progression was like a wall of water flattening everything in its path. 'How can I consider marriage, *cara*, when I can think of no woman but you?'

Her eyes widened. 'Oh, Luca,' she whispered. *Dio.* 'I should not say such things.' He shot to his feet. 'I promised that you would be safe from my attentions and I meant it. I will bid you goodnight.'

He'd not taken two steps before soft fingers circled his arm, pulling him to a halt. He dragged in a ragged breath. 'Monique, what are you doing?'

'I don't know. I…'

Her eyes reflected both his turmoil and his hunger. 'I can promise you nothing,' he growled. 'You should run from me as fast as you can.'

Her chin lifted. 'Can you promise me friendship?'

He stilled. 'Always.'

She reached up on tiptoe then as if to kiss him, but he held her off. 'Do you know what you are doing?'

'Following my instincts…my desires. Now that you've removed the spectre of the other woman—and, yes, I know she was hypothetical, this woman you talked about marrying, but she still felt real to me—it leaves me free now to do what I've been longing to do. To kiss you, Luca. And more. Without guilt.'

His hands curled about her arms. He had to fight against the urge to draw her near. 'You deserve more. You—'

'What if I don't want more?' she whispered. 'Luca, both of our lives are in flux at the moment.

Neither one of us is in a position to make those kinds of promises.'

Did she mean that? He tried to concentrate over the stampede of hunger her words sent raging through him. What if *he* wanted more?

'No promises beyond friendship. And no regrets.'

If they had friendship; if they had trust…what more could he want? He was so tired of watching his every move, weighing his every action, and more than anything he wanted to lose himself in this woman and live in the moment.

She drew back, uncertainty flickering in her eyes. 'If I've made a mistake, misread what you wanted, I'm sorry. I thought—' She broke off, swallowing. 'How awkward. If I've made you feel uncomfortable, I apologise. I—'

He reached out and touched a finger to her lips. 'You're not mistaken, *il mio cuore*. I want you with every fibre of my being, but I am no longer an impulsive youth. Also, I keep feeling the need to pinch myself. I keep thinking I'm going to wake, and you'll be gone.'

She stared so deeply into his eyes he felt she must touch his very soul, and then she smiled, and his heart stopped beating for a moment before giving a giant kick. 'I'm not going anywhere, Luca.'

He allowed himself, finally, a totally male, totally wolfish smile. 'I am going to make such love to you that your knees will go weak and your bones will turn to water.'

Her breath hitched and quickened.

'I hunger to hear your name on your lips when—'

It was her hand on his lips this time, halting his words, and she gave a shaky laugh. 'Shut up and kiss me already.'

In answer, he lifted her into his arms and started for the stairs. 'Once I start kissing you, *cara*, I do not want to stop. And while the sofas are comfortable, if Fern were to come looking for you…'

'Good point.' She pressed a series of kisses along his jawline and the light sensual touch drew his muscles tight. 'I don't want Fern knowing about us, Luca.'

He halted halfway up the stairs to stare at her.

'She's only three and she's had more upheaval in her short life than anyone should ever have. I don't want anything to upset her current equilibrium.'

He nodded slowly. Their children's welfare must come first. 'I would never do anything to purposely hurt or upset Fern.' He'd grown increasingly fond of the little girl.

'I know.'

She tunnelled her fingers through his hair and this time her touch was neither soft nor tentative. It was sure and urgent. And somehow carnal. It had him imagining those hands on his body and—

He stumbled.

'Maybe it's me who'll make your knees weak,' she murmured, her teeth tugging gently on his earlobe.

Gritting his teeth, he made it to his bedroom and set her gently on her feet before closing the door silently behind them. Turning back, he went to gather her in his arms, but she held him off. 'I want to see you.'

Her voice was a husky whisper that brushed against nerve-endings already taut with need and he had to bite back a groan, but he submitted to her request without murmur. When she seized the hem of his T-shirt and lifted it, he raised his arms and let her draw it over his head.

She dropped the shirt to the floor, took a step back, one hand going to her mouth. Moonlight flooded the room from the two enormous windows on the adjacent walls and he watched her eyes widen in awed appreciation and couldn't stop his shoulders from going back and his chest from puffing out. When she looked at him like that, he felt he could take on the world.

Kicking herself forward again, she unbuttoned his jeans and eased them and his briefs down his hips and legs. He stepped out of them and she rose, staring, her eyes roving over his body before she lifted her gaze to his face. 'You're beautiful, Luca.' She moistened her lips. 'The most beautiful man I've ever seen. Beautiful all the way through.'

It took all his strength not to drag her into his arms and ravage her then and there. First, though, he wanted to see her naked too, but he sensed an edge of shyness in her that made him curb his impatience.

Pulling her gently to him, he pressed kisses to the corner of her mouth, working his way along her jaw to the line of her neck, taking his time until her head dropped back on a sigh to give him as much access as he desired. Only then did he ease the T-shirt from the waistband of her shorts and pull it over her head. Flicking open the clasp of her bra, he eased it from her body as he bit gently down on her earlobe.

Rather than reaching for her breasts and cupping them in his hands, he splayed his hands across her back and pressed her against him, the friction of their bodies feeding the wildfire of desire burning between them. And as she slowly turned to him more fully, he felt a sense of privilege he'd never before experienced.

Her hands explored the shape of his shoulders, the muscles in his back, and all the while she pressed kisses to his collarbone and the base of his throat. His entire frame started to shake with his effort to hold himself back. He refused to gobble and devour like a greedy wolf. Instead, he danced his fingers down her spine to her waist. When he and Monique finally came together, he wanted her as hungry and mindless as him.

Her mouth closed over one of his nipples and his body jerked, the sensation shooting straight to his groin. *Dio*, this woman! Sliding his hands up her sides, he grazed her nipples with his thumbs.

Her gasp and the way she arched into his touch encouraged him to repeat the action, again and again. 'Luca, please...' His name seemed to be drawn from the very depths of her and only then did he cup her breasts, lowering his mouth to lathe the tight buds of her nipples with his tongue until she was clinging to his shoulders, her breath sawing in and out.

Easing back slightly and trying to steady his breathing, he caught her gaze. Lowering his hands to the waistband of her shorts, he very gently eased them over her hips. Kneeling before her, he pressed a kiss to her stomach as he lowered her panties down her legs as well. Lifting each foot by the ankle, he eased her clothes away so she wouldn't become tangled in them.

He knelt there and gazed up at her. '*Cara*, you are exquisite.'

She stared up at him with wide eyes full of need and a vulnerability that almost undid him. 'I've never wanted anyone the way I want you, Luca,' she whispered. 'Please tell me you have protection.'

Her words were breathless and raw, and he gave up fighting the need pouring through him. 'In the bedside drawer,' he growled, lifting her onto the bed and falling down beside her. Their mouths finally met in a kiss of fierce ardour and equally fierce tenderness. That tidal surge of desire picked them up in its current and hurtled them into a maelstrom of pleasure and sensation.

He explored her every inch, and she explored his—with hunger, delight…joy. Their cries and moans mingled until he didn't know where he finished and she began, but all the time they moved closer and closer towards a pinnacle higher than any other he'd ever before scaled.

Until, with a cry, Monique hurtled from its heights, her body arching into his, her muscles clenching around him, and he followed, soaring into an explosion of colour and sensation that left him floating gently to earth and feeling as if he'd been remade into a new man—one of steel and diamonds and sunlight.

He rolled them over, shaping her to his side. *'Dio!'* He could barely catch his breath. He told her he thought her beautiful, amazing, magnificent.

Her soft laugh was warmth personified. 'I've no idea what you're saying, Luca. But I suspect I agree. That was… There aren't words in the English language adequate enough to describe it.'

She nestled into his side and Luca drifted off

into a dream-free sleep, wondering if he'd ever before in his life felt such a complete sense of well-being.

Luca woke to soft morning sunshine and the sounds of birds chattering in the vines outside. Without opening his eyes, he reached for Monique, but his arms came back empty. He sat up with a frown.

Her side of the bed was empty. Monique had gone.

Rubbing a hand over his heart, he forced himself back down to the pillows. It didn't mean anything was wrong. It didn't mean she regretted last night.

One of the children might have needed her. He swallowed. Or she might simply prefer to sleep in her own bed.

Friendship and no regrets, that's all they'd promised each other. He stared at the ceiling, replaying last night's lovemaking in his mind, and slowly his tension eased. Monique wouldn't regret what they'd shared. She'd hold it close—a cherished memory—just as he did. As for friendship, surely that had only been strengthened by what they'd shared.

Monique wouldn't go back on their promises. Yet none of that eased his disappointment at not waking beside her this morning.

If he'd needed reassurance, the smile she sent

him when he walked into the kitchen a short while later gave it to him, as did her cheery, 'Good morning.'

He checked the impulse to kiss her. Both Fern and Benito were at the breakfast bar, eating their breakfast. He swooped down to give his son a kiss and ruffled Fern's hair before planting himself on the one remaining stool and pulling a packet of cereal towards him. Monique handed him the milk and nibbled a piece of toast.

'What do you three have planned for the day?'

Monique started and a faint pink stained her cheeks. Had she been remembering last night? How long did he have to wait before he could have his wicked way with her again?

'We thought we might go exploring.'

'I want to go down to the river,' Fern told him solemnly.

River? 'Do you mean the stream at the bottom of the hill?'

Fern nodded her little head hard. 'I want to go swimming.'

'It's not deep enough for swimming, I'm afraid. It's only ankle deep.'

She cocked her head to one side. 'So I could paddle?'

'You can paddle,' Monique agreed.

'It's further than it looks,' he warned.

'I'll pop Benny in his stroller, then. The path down looks sturdy enough.'

True, but her arms would get tired, pushing it back up the hill again. And what of Fern and her little legs?

'Would you like to join us?' Monique asked, as if reading his mind, her eyes dancing, and he had to fight the urge to reach across and drag her mouth to his. 'Or do you have to work?'

'I have to work.'

Her face fell.

'But maybe I could work this afternoon instead and take the morning off.'

Her smile and Fern's cheer were his rewards. After all, he told himself, it'd only be for a couple of hours. And Monique might need help with the children.

Ninety minutes later he found himself sitting on the bank of the little stream in the shade of a linden tree. Fern happily paddled while Benito sat on the blanket beside Monique, attempting to eat a banana but mashing most of it between his fingers.

'I missed you this morning,' he said in a low voice as Monique wiped banana from Benito's leg.

She glanced up. 'I'm sorry. I just thought it'd be best if I slept in my own bed.' She glanced at Fern. 'In case someone came looking for me.'

It made perfect sense. It shouldn't chafe at him so.

'Is everything okay?'

Her soft question snapped him back. '*Sì*, it is perfect, *cara*.'

'Auntie Mon, when will Benny walk properly so he can paddle too?'

'Probably not for another couple of months, pumpkin.'

The little girl frowned. 'And he's too little to swim yet.'

'Ah, but think of the fun we'll have when Benny's older and comes for holidays to Mirror Glass Bay. You'll be able to teach him to swim.'

When she returned to Mirror Glass Bay? He fought a frown. Of course she would eventually return there. It was her home.

Fern jumped up and down, clapping her hands. 'Come and paddle with me, Luca!'

He shot to his feet. Somewhere along the line, Fern had won him over with her shy smile and enchanting sense of humour. He was hers to command as she pleased.

Monique stripped Benito to his nappy and soon followed.

He allowed Monique's laughter, Benny's squeals of delight and Fern's chatter to ease the burning in his soul. He didn't know what the future held, but for today he would simply live in the moment.

# CHAPTER TEN

THE REST OF the week and most of the next passed in a haze of fun and sensual delight. Monique had never known such peace and happiness. Luca continued to work, and work hard, she suspected, but he'd do his best to spend at least a morning or afternoon each day with her and the children. They'd amble around the vineyard, discovering hidden nooks, and have picnics beside the grapevines. Other times they visited the nearby town and ambled along its cobbled streets, eating gelatos.

And at night she and Luca made love—learning each other's bodies, discovering what gave the greatest pleasure, and talking into the wee small hours. She hadn't known a lover could be as giving as Luca, as patient and sensitive...as skilled.

She swallowed. For as long as they remained here at Casa Speranza—Home of Hope—it felt as if nothing bad could ever happen. It felt as if they were contained in their own little bubble where the real world couldn't touch them.

It was an illusion. A foolish fancy. As was the hope that had grown in her heart, despite her best efforts to prune it into submission.

Casa Speranza—Home of Hope—and she had a heart of hope. It would all end in tears—her tears. Yet she couldn't find it in her to regret a single moment of her time with Luca. It's not as if she'd meant to fall in love with him.

In her weakest moments she'd imagine Luca finding a way to fit her into his world. After all, he'd found a solution to Fern's situation so easily. Couldn't he do the same for them?

If he wanted to, he could.

She made herself face that fact with eyes wide open. If Luca wanted to pursue a permanent relationship with her, he could.

But, despite all her romantic foolishness, she was a realist. Just because he'd decided against making a cold marriage of convenience, it didn't mean he'd be prepared to marry a girl with the kind of family Monique had. Her mother and sister would be a thorn in his side forever—wanting money, threatening and probably giving entirely false exposés to the tabloids.

God! The thought made her own stomach churn and she had nothing left to lose at their hands. But Luca had everything to lose. He was trying so hard to redeem and reclaim his family's good name. Marrying her wouldn't help him achieve that. In fact, it'd probably hinder it.

'Impossible,' she told herself for the hundredth time. Anything beyond a temporary affair was impossible.

'It's all set,' Luca told her, late in their second week. 'The trap has been laid and now all we need to do is watch and wait. Soon we will know who the guilty culprits are.'

Everything inside her drew tight at his words, at the determination gleaming in his eyes. She knew then, even before he spoke again, that their idyll at Casa Speranza was at an end. 'That's excellent news.' She made herself smile. 'Once you've dealt with the culprits, you and Rosetta can finally move forward.'

He nodded.

'I'm happy for you, Luca.' And she meant it. 'You've worked hard to uncover this conspiracy. When do we leave for Rome?'

'In the morning.'

'I'll make sure we're packed and ready.'

She played with the children. She kept the smile on her face. She refused to let her internal disquiet ruin the peace and contentment they'd all found here. But that night their lovemaking took on a desperate edge.

Afterwards, when they were lying side by side, both panting from their exertions, he gripped her hand. 'When we return to Rome…'

He didn't finish the sentence, but she knew

what he wanted to say. Only he didn't know how to say it. She took the initiative from him. 'If we want to continue our affair—'

'I most definitely do. Do not be in any doubt of that, *cara*.'

So did she. If she were a sensible woman, she'd end it now. But apparently she wasn't a sensible woman. 'Then we keep it just between us. We keep it secret.'

He didn't say anything for several long moments. She wanted him to argue. She wanted him to make their relationship public…official.

'Yes,' he finally said. 'Secret. Our business and nobody else's.'

Her heart sank, though. She was a fool for wanting more. She refused to let her chin drop. He had enough people already pressuring him into taking this direction or that. She refused to join their number.

'It'll be for the best,' she forced herself to say. She didn't need anyone else to witness her humiliation and heartache when the time came.

'I wish we could stay here forever.'

It wasn't the same as wanting her forever, though, was it? 'Me too,' she found herself whispering back anyway.

They made love again—fierce, hungry, wild love. Tonight, though, she didn't wait until he fell asleep before she left his bed.

* * *

Monique and the children barely saw Luca over the course of the next five days. Oh, he popped up to the nursery for an hour each evening. And two of the five nights he'd taken her to his room, where they'd made love with as much fervour as ever, but she couldn't help feeling he was slipping away from her. The real world—*his* real world—had started to reclaim him.

And she missed him more than she could say.

Not that he took up all her thoughts. She loved spending her days with Fern and Benny. The children could be a handful—they were growing fast—but they were an absolute joy. Her life was blessed. She reminded herself of that over and over, counted those blessings every single day.

The garden was their favourite haunt. They spent much of their days tumbling on the lawn, exploring the gardens and playing. To stop Fern from missing the delights of Casa Speranza too keenly, Monique had created a game that was a combination of croquet, skittles and basketball, though they used soft mallets and foam balls, plastic rather than wooden skittles, and a waist-high basketball hoop.

It was Fern's favourite game, and as Benny's favourite thing was crawling after Fern, it kept them entertained for ages. Especially when she taught Fern a couple of Italian songs and they sang them as they played. Benny clapped his hands and joined in the best he could.

They were in the midst of one such fast and furious game when a voice—full of laughter and longing—said, 'You look as if you're having the most splendid fun.'

*Luca.*

Benny crawled over and demanded, 'Up! Up!'

Fern raced over and flung her arms around his legs.

He picked Benny up and rested a hand on Fern's hair, glancing down with a smile so gentle Monique's heart clenched at the picture they made.

At the picture *he* made.

Would he one day re-create this idyll of family and belonging with another woman, a woman from his world? The thought was a knife to her heart.

Fern handed him the croquet mallet. 'Come and play too.'

Snapping to, Monique settled her game face into place and pointed to a ball. 'First you have to negotiate the croquet course before knocking down all the skittles, and then shooting a hoop.'

As Luca played, his usual seriousness gave way to a sense of playfulness that had both children chortling and wanting to be close to him.

'Benny's too little to play it properly.' Fern's little shoulders drooped on her sigh.

'But it's a game we can play when we're back home in Mirror Glass Bay,' Monique reminded her.

The little girl brightened. 'So we can play it with him when he's a big boy of three like me.'

Behind Fern's back, Luca frowned, but Monique did her best to ignore it. That frown meant nothing. 'Exactly! Which will be loads and oodles and gazillions of fun.'

'Oodles and gazillions!' Fern giggled, before rounding back on Luca 'Teach us a song,' she demanded. 'Please,' she added as a hurried afterthought when Monique raised a pointed eyebrow.

He started to sing, but Fern interrupted him. 'Auntie Mon has already taught us that one.'

He turned to Monique, that tantalising mouth dropping open, sending a giddy rush of excitement surging through her.

'In Italian?'

'*Sì.*' She nodded. 'Let's show him, Fern.'

They all sang the song, and then Luca taught them another. Benny had started to rub his eyes, his head drooping before starting awake again. Monique was about to suggest it was time to return to the house when at that exact moment a fat raindrop landed on her head.

She glanced up and gulped at the dark clouds that had gathered overhead. More fat drops fell. They'd been so intent on their game she'd not noticed the sky darkening. They were at one of the furthest points from the house too. They'd be drenched before they reached it.

'Come on.' Luca reached down and pulled her to

'I care for her too! I...*love* her.' His words were low and vehement. 'I will always make time for her.' His gaze softened at whatever he saw in her face and he reached across and took her hand. 'This I promise you, Monique.'

It would help to mediate the damage already done, but it wouldn't undo it completely. She needed to start curtailing the amount of time Fern and Luca spent together.

'I had fun playing your game earlier.'

He kept hold of her hand and it made her blood dance through her veins.

He frowned, as if trying to work out a difficult puzzle. 'It would not be that fun with anyone else.'

His words startled a laugh from her. 'Of course not. Fern and Benito are the best children in the world.'

'I meant you.'

The look he sent her made her heart falter.

'I meant no other woman could have made that game so much fun.' His frowned deepened. 'No other woman could ever love Fern and Benny the way that you do.'

Was he saying what she thought he was saying? Her heart beat so hard it almost hurt.

'Stay,' he said, turning to her with an earnest intensity that smashed through every barrier she'd to erect around her heart.

'ay?'

what capacity? Her heart thundered in her

her feet, thrusting Benny into her arms and catching Fern up in his. 'The summerhouse is nearby. We can shelter there until the storm passes.'

'It's locked,' Fern told him.

He grinned. 'But I know where the key is kept.'

Fern had been dying to get inside the summerhouse with its indoor pool visible through the myriad windows ever since they'd discovered it. Monique owned to a sliver of anticipation too. It had looked wonderful from the outside when they'd peered through the windows.

'Princess Fern has been wondering how to get into the enchanted glass palace.'

Luca reached above the doorframe for the key, unlocked the door and ushered them all inside. 'As long as Princess Fern has her Auntie Monique with her, she can visit any time she wishes to.'

Monique couldn't help smiling when Fern cheered and wriggled to get down.

'I love you, King Luca,' Fern yelled as she raced towards the pool.

'No running,' Monique called after her. 'And be careful near the edge. I don't want you falling in and taking an unnecessary dip. Promise me?' she persisted. Her niece could be a little monkey when it came to the water.

'I promise, Auntie Mon!'

Only then did Monique fall down onto a banana lounge and try to control the pounding of her heart. *I love you, King Luca.* What had she been thinking, allowing Fern to grow so close to Luca? She thought she'd been doing enough, reminding Fern that their time in Italy was finite, that they'd be returning to Mirror Glass Bay… without Benny and Luca.

It obviously hadn't been enough. She should have been more vigilant! How could she have let this happen? Fern had suffered enough separation in her short life.

She eased back as Benny snuggled in against her chest. He'd be asleep in two minutes flat. She glanced across at Luca, who still stood by the door as if frozen to the spot. Her heart pounded. She had to mitigate the damage. Somehow.

Luca swung towards her, his eyes dazed, before he lowered himself to the lounge beside her. *'Dio…'* he murmured. 'Did you hear what Fern said to me?'

*All too clearly.*

She nodded. The stunned expression in his eyes made all the sore places inside her ache.

His mouth worked. 'Are children always so reckless with their hearts?'

'Not reckless, generous,' she corrected. She glanced at her niece, her heart aching. 'They haven't learned to be guarded yet.'

'It is terrifying! How do we keep them from getting hurt?'

'We can't. It's impossible.' Though her heart clenched at the thought. 'Nobody gets through

life without getting their heart bruised.' She made herself smile. 'We just do our best to be a soft place for them to land.'

She fought the urge to reach across and clasp his hand. 'We do our best, Luca. That's all we can do.'

He stared at her and she had to swallow the temptation that trickled through her. Now wasn't the time to get caught up in the shape of his lips or the breadth of his shoulders. Or that lazy slumbrous look in his eyes.

She forced her gaze back to Fern, who was busy making a circuit around the summerhouse to stare out of each window in turn. She moistened suddenly dry lips. 'While we're on that subject…'

He leaned towards her, and his amber scent drifted across to play havoc with her senses. 'Yes?'

'When I return to Australia there'll be a lot video calls to keep us all connected, yes? S Benny doesn't forget me, so he knows I hav forgotten him.'

*'Sì.'*

'I'll always make time for him.'

'I know this, yes. You love him.'

'I have a favour to ask. When Fern return to Australia, will you make a l Fern? I know you've no legal or m to her.' She smoothed a hand dow pressed a kiss to the top of his h ing Luca's gaze again. 'But sh and I don't want her feeling h

ears. Had he found a way to make a relationship between them work? Had he—?

A sudden splash broke the silence. Before Monique had even registered that Fern had fallen into the pool, Luca was on his feet and had dived into the pool, fully clothed, to lift up a spluttering Fern.

The little girl blinked water from her eyes. 'Why did you dive in wearing all your clothes, Luca?'

'To rescue you.'

'But I can swim. See? The water's warm, Aunty Mon!'

Monique subsided back into the banana lounge, readjusting Benny against her shoulder. Her mind was a whirl of confusion as Luca ushered Fern out of the pool, found towels and dry clothes for them—a sweater that came down past Fern's knees—and snacks. Soon Fern had fallen asleep on the cushions she'd piled beside Monique's lounge.

Luca had dressed in tracksuit pants and a T, and he looked casual and virile and more tempting than ever, but a storm to rival the one outside raged in his eyes.

Because he wanted her to stay? She couldn't prevent the leap her heart gave.

'*Dio!*' he bit out, his voice low, his hands clenched. 'I thought Fern...'

She suddenly realised the emotion in his eyes was fear. And it wasn't for Monique but for

Fern. There was nothing of the lover in his gaze, nothing of…

How many different ways could she call herself a fool? With an effort she swallowed and nodded. 'I'm sorry she frightened you.'

'Frightened? She terrified me! I thought…' He seemed to rein himself in before letting out a long breath. 'She can swim?'

'I live near the beach. I've been getting her lessons since she was six months old.'

He was silent for a long moment and then nodded as if coming to a decision. 'I meant what I said before. I want you to stay.'

Reality rose up to smack her in the face with cold, hard sense and her heart shrivelled to the size of a cold, hard pebble. 'You want me to stay as Benny's nanny.' It wasn't even a question.

'You love Benny and care for him as no other woman could. And if you stay, I can keep an eye on Fern, keep her safe and—'

'*No!*'

His head rocked back at her vehemence. 'What have I done, *cara*? What have I said wrong?'

She tried to rein in her raging emotions. What she needed to do—the solution that had been staring her in the face since Fern had told Luca she loved him—hit her now. She just hadn't wanted to face it. 'I can't stay, Luca. I'm sorry. In fact… I can't stay here in Rome any longer. I need to return to Australia immediately.'

His eyes went suddenly wild. 'What do you mean? You promised me a year. There are months yet before your scheduled return to Australia.'

'Benny is settled and happy here. He loves you and Anna is great with him. He'll be fine without me.'

'But—'

'Fern has come to rely on you too much and I need to nip that in the bud now, before she's in danger of being hurt even more.'

'That is not necessary. It—'

'Do you see a future for us, Luca?' She broke in over the top of him. 'You and me and the children as a proper family?'

He paled and she could see it wasn't a scenario he'd considered. 'We made no promises to each other,' he said in a low voice.

She made herself smile, even as her heart shattered into a million jagged pieces. 'We promised friendship and no regrets, Luca, and if I'm to keep that promise I need to call a halt to all of this and return home.'

'Can you not give me time to consider what you're asking? I...'

She'd started to shake her head even before he trailed off. 'If I stay, Luca, I'm going to start wanting more from you. I'm going to fall in love with you.'

He flinched. She hadn't thought she could hurt more than she already did. That flinch proved her wrong. 'Look, the storm's passed.' She refused to focus on the pain. She didn't want to break down in front of him. She pushed to her feet. 'It's time to take the children back to the house.'

Luca strode into the grand perfection of the Villa Vieri, but the dwelling held no more cheer for him now than it had when he'd been a child. In another two days Monique and Fern would be gone and what happiness he'd started to associate with the place would likewise be gone.

His hands clenched. He didn't want her to go, but that didn't mean he loved her. *It didn't.* He'd been mistaken about love once before. Camilla hadn't loved him and yet he'd been so sure and certain. He didn't *think* Monique would try to manipulate him, but wasn't her declaration just another form of manipulation? Just as Camilla's had been?

He refused to trust his instincts. And before he did anything as earth shattering as propose marriage to a woman, he needed to speak to his grandfather and reconcile the older man to *everything*.

At least he and Rosetta had uncovered the traitor within their ranks. Today they'd finally emerged victorious. Only victory hadn't tasted sweet. The fight had been dirty, ugly…and far from edifying.

Nonetheless his parents, one aunt and uncle, and a perfidious cousin who'd been cowed by his parents, had resigned from the board. Once the lawyers had provided the guilty parties with the evidence of their culpability, a collection of the various contracts bearing forgeries of Luca's signature, not to mention the recorded conversation Rosetta had made—Rosetta, who they'd thought they'd won to their side—they'd had no option but to step down or risk facing criminal charges.

Rosetta and he were now joint CEOs. From this day forward they would share the burden, responsibility and privilege of leading the Vieri Corporation into the future. He should be happy, over the moon, exultant.

Instead, he felt flat, demoralised…exhausted.

When he entered the nursery, he found Monique holding a sleeping Benito in her arms, tears pouring down her cheeks.

'I'm sorry,' she hiccupped when she saw him standing there. 'I can't seem to stop.'

Friendship and no regrets. *He* could at least keep *his* word.

Very gently he took the baby from her and placed him in his cot, and then pulled her into his arms, stroking her back as silent sobs racked her. His heart clenched. She had always understood how difficult the parting would be from her godson, but that had not stopped her loving him with her whole heart.

She could stay. She didn't need to leave. He— He shook the thought off. He couldn't ask her to stay. He owed his allegiance to the family corporation and his grandfather. And she deserved more than to be a guilty secret he kept hidden away. She was right to want to leave.

'I wish I could make this easier for you, *il mio cuore.*'

She pulled away, wiped her eyes, and gave him a brave smile that had a groan rising through him. 'What does that mean...*il mio cuore?* I keep meaning to look it up.'

'My heart,' he murmured, his collar tightening about his throat. 'It is like saying sweetheart or darling in English.'

'My heart,' she repeated. 'Such an expression should be more than a casual endearment.'

Something deep inside him tensed. Would an honourable man, a truly honourable man let this woman go?

Or would keeping her merely prove that he was made in his parents' image—selfishly taking want he wanted without a thought for who it might be hurting?

He took a step back. He refused to be that man. Monique was right to leave. He and Benito would be perfectly fine without her.

'I need to thank you. You organised drug and alcohol counselling for Skye and my mother. While my mother has declined the offer, Skye hasn't. She emailed me to let me know.'

He blinked at the change of subject. 'Something you said made me realise I'd thrown my money around recklessly. I wanted to do what I could to mitigate any potential damage I'd done.'

He was an honourable man. And he had every intention of remaining that way. 'Is there anything you need? Anything I can do to help?'

She searched his face, but very slowly the light in her eyes died and her gaze dropped. 'I don't think so, but thanks for asking.' She gestured at Benito, who was starting to stir. 'I'll leave you to have some quality time with your son.'

With those words she turned and left.

And he refused to call her back.

Luca's grandfather arrived ten days after Monique and Fern left. Luca had done his best to shore up the hole that yawned through the centre of him with their absence. It would take time to adjust, he told himself for the hundredth time. That was all.

But how much time would it take? It'd already been ten days and yet his yearning for Monique continued to grow.

'Your cousin will eventually marry and have babies, Luca, and her mind and attention will wander,' his grandfather said over breakfast the next morning. 'No good will come of this, I warn you.'

Luca brushed a hand across his eyes and forced his mind back to the discussion at hand. 'What if it is my mind that is wandering because of Benito? I want to spend more time with my son.'

For the first time it occurred to him how much his grandfather had sacrificed in ensuring the Vieri Corporation's continued success. 'How much time did you spend with my mother and her siblings when they were growing up, Nonno?'

Did he regret the sacrifices he'd made?

'There was no time for that. Men did not concern themselves with such things. I made sure my family wanted for nothing! That was my job, and I did it well.'

Luca's heart started to thump. Before he'd discovered he had a son, before he'd experienced the love a man could have for his child, he might have believed his grandfather's words, but now...

'As soon as you find a suitable wife, you too will be in a better position to once again focus all your energies where they're most needed and get your priorities into order.'

'Benito *is* my first priority.'

The older man's face darkened. 'You were a fool to get that girl pregnant, Luca. We could've kept everything so simple.'

He stared at his grandfather and his heart started to pound. Cold, hard dread flooded his chest. 'It was you.' The words were out before he could stop them, but the realisation had him abandoning his customary caution.

'What are you talking about?'

'It was you who paid Anita off.' As he spoke the words, he knew his suspicion was right.

His grandfather looked as if he was about to deny it, but in the end he merely shrugged. 'I did what was necessary.'

'How did you find out about Benito?'

'Piero. He intercepted the emails and sent them to me. You forget he was my personal assistant before he became yours. He knew I would know how to act for the best.'

'For the best?' Luca started to shake in an effort to contain the rage that threatened to burst from him.

'Do not look at me like that. I had only your best interests in mind. You and Bella were so close to marrying!' He spread his hands as if that explained everything. 'As soon as you were safely married, I had every intention of telling you about the child. Benito's mother was insisting on it. I only got her co-operation when I explained to her how important this marriage was.' He huffed as if pleased with himself. 'She did not wish to create trouble in your life.'

Monique had been right about Anita. She'd had integrity and honesty and decency. And his grandfather had taken advantage of it.

'I made sure she had the means to support both herself and the child in the meantime.'

He'd thought his grandfather had loved him, but now...

His grandfather's face turned purple as if he read that thought in Luca's face. 'We were working so hard to bring Gianni's back into the fold, where it belongs. I know you want that as much as I do!'

Luca rose to his feet, his mind racing. 'You who have spoken to me so often of honour... What you've done is the antithesis of honour.' He had to battle the nausea churning through him. 'You don't care about honour or respectability. You just want the appearance of it.'

The older man slammed his hand on the table again. 'It is the same thing!'

Luca realised he had been in danger of following a set of values that beneath their pretty veneer were rotten to the core. In making a good marriage, he'd been trying to buy a family name... to buy respectability. But what was respectable about such a cold-blooded exchange?

Nothing.

Not one of the people here at Villa Vieri—not his parents or his grandfather—cared what Luca wanted or what would make him happy. The only person who'd cared was Monique. And he'd let her go.

His heart pounded. Had he left it too late?

There was only one way to find out. He turned and strode from the room.

# CHAPTER ELEVEN

THE WAVES ROLLED up onto the shore of Mirror Glass Bay's glorious beach with the mildness of a grandmother handing out cookies to apple-cheeked children. Monique scowled at it. She wanted tempestuous thundering surf and sand-blasting winds. She wanted the beach to reflect the turmoil roiling within her.

For the four hundred and eighty-third time since arriving back in Mirror Glass Bay nearly a fortnight ago, she told herself she had no right to such emotions. What, after all, did she have to complain about? She had everything she'd wanted—or had said she'd wanted—two months ago.

She had Fern.

What was more, she had two part-time jobs that paid the bills, and was working towards a qualification that would lead to financial security and career satisfaction. What more could she want?

She kicked a hank of seaweed. *Luca.* She wanted Luca. How stupid was that?

'Not stupid,' she muttered, stomping in the water and trying to spray it as far and wide as she could. It was out of season, so she practically had the beach to herself. Which meant she could stomp as much as she wanted without inconveniencing anyone.

It wasn't *stupid* to want Luca. The man was a Greek god, a Renaissance work of art, a masterpiece of masculinity—broad, lean, powerful and magnetically handsome. Plus, he was a lover unlike any other. What red-blooded heterosexual woman wouldn't want him?

Except her want went so much deeper. She missed Luca—the man she could talk to, joke with and sit silently with—in the same way she'd miss a limb. A constant gnawing ache sat like lead in her chest, a persistent reminder that he no longer featured on the everyday landscape of her life. And adjusting to that felt like adapting to having lost an arm or a leg.

It made no sense. Yet it made total sense.

It was the man inside the beautiful packaging that she truly hungered for. The man who rarely laughed, but when he did managed to light up an entire room. The man who saw an injustice and moved heaven and earth to fix it. A man for whom honour and duty weren't just empty words.

She halted, covering her face with her hands.

A moment later she forced them back down to her sides. The cold hard truth was that Luca didn't feel the same way about her. If he had, he wouldn't have let her go. But he had. So easily.

Tugging her T-shirt over her head and shrugging out of her shorts, she strode into the water and dived under an irritatingly gentle wave, the water temperature too mild to steal her breath. She closed her eyes and tried to let the gentle swell ease the burn in her soul. For a little while it did. The rhythmic ebb and flow, the rise and fall of the waves and the absence of a breeze soothed and hypnotised. Until a playful wave splashed her face.

Opening her eyes, she glanced shoreward and saw a lone dark-haired figure moving along its length towards her. Everything inside her stiffened. *Luca?*

'Oh, for goodness' sake.' She made her voice deliberately mocking. 'Now she's seeing him in every dark-haired man who crosses her path.'

She started swimming parallel to the shore. An exhausted body helped her sleep at night and swimming for forty minutes a day certainly qualified as exhausting.

She allowed herself the briefest of smiles. She'd thought heartbreak was supposed to make you either fat from all the ice-cream-consuming comfort eating you did or emaciate you with grief. Not her. She was going to be disgustingly toned and healthy.

Which was just as well, she lectured herself

as she stroked through the water, trying to find a rhythm that would momentarily quieten all the noise in her mind. She was the legal guardian of a young girl. She needed to be a good role model.

Her strokes slowed. A young girl who was constantly asking when Benny and Luca were coming to visit.

There'd been a couple of quick video calls—Luca was as good as his word. And Monique had been doing her best to keep Fern's mind occupied so the little girl wouldn't pine. The effort left her exhausted most evenings, but she did what she could to push her own heartbreak to one side. It was Fern's welfare that mattered most.

And the heartbreak was Monique's own fault.

Although Fern missed Benny and Luca, she'd adjusted to being back in Mirror Glass Bay remarkably well. Monique had worried her niece would fear Skye arriving to take her away again. Fern had checked once that her mother wasn't coming for her, but after Monique's assurances to the contrary it seemed the little girl had banished such fears from her mind.

Which was great. She was glad Fern had started to feel so secure. Now she just had to work on reducing the number of Benny and Luca questions that continued to arrive daily.

She forced herself to keep doggedly ploughing through the water and *not* notice the man on the beach. As he drew closer, though, she darted another glance in his direction and nearly sank. He even walked like Luca!

Halting by her clothes and towel, the man pulled his shirt over his head and shucked off his shorts to reveal swimming trunks that hung low on his hips and clung to strong, powerful thighs. Her mouth dried. Every red-blooded cell sprang to life. Dear God. That *was* Luca!

She hadn't been imagining anything! That was Luca. *In the flesh*. Oh, and what flesh…

Her feet touched bottom, but the sand kept shifting beneath them. Luca strode into the water and dived under a wave. He reached her in less than a dozen easy strokes of those powerful arms, biceps flexing in a way that made her dash cold seawater on her face. Except there wasn't water cold enough to dampen the heat rising through her.

Before she could temper her shock or the desire raging through her, he stood in front of her.

'Hello, *cara*.'

'Hello, *il mio cuore*,' she whispered, the endearment slipping out as if it were the most natural thing in the world. But those words—*il mio cuore*—had featured in her dreams and she was powerless to stop them.

He smiled, one of those rare, beautiful smiles, and it took every atom of strength she had not to fling her arms around his neck.

'It is good to see you, Monique. My eyes have been hungry for the sight of you.'

'You…' She swallowed. *Keep it together.* 'You saw me just a few days ago on our last video call.'

'Pah!' He waved a hand, his nose wrinkling in disgust. 'That does not count.'

It didn't? Her heart raced and she gave up trying to get it back under control. 'What are you doing here, Luca? I—' A terrible thought hit her. 'Benny? Is Benny—?'

'Benny is happy and healthy and currently sleeping in his old room a few streets away, with Anna keeping watch.' His eyes darkened. 'I had to come.'

'Why?'

'I wanted to make sure all was well with you.'

'You didn't have to travel halfway around the world to do that.'

One finger reached out to trail a path down her cheek. 'I needed to see your face when I told you I missed you.'

Her heart pounded so hard she was amazed that agitated waves weren't rippling all around her. 'Me or Benny's nanny?' If he thought they were one and the same—

He smiled. 'I miss you as Benito's nanny, it is true. But mostly I miss you as my lover.'

She leaned towards him, tried to read the expression in his eyes. She told herself she'd be a fool to believe him, but… Luca had never played games with her. He'd only ever been kind and honest.

'Really?' She reached up to touch his cheek, but a wave pushed her into him, and her hands splayed across his chest instead. 'Oops, I—'

His hands went about her waist to steady her and her words dried.

'Yes, really,' he answered, as if their proximity had no effect on him at all.

The tight line of his jaw betrayed otherwise. She stared at the pulse thumping in his throat in fascination. If she touched her lips to that spot, would he show her how much he'd missed her?

'I want to be the good man you think me, Monique.'

She blinked herself back into the moment, frowned. 'You're already a good man.'

'I know we promised friendship and no regrets...' his hands tightened on her waist '...but I regret letting you go, *tesoro mio*.'

He regretted...? Her brain short-circuited. She opened her mouth, but no sound came out.

'And I wanted to know if you too maybe had regrets and if, maybe, you missed me a little?'

Her heart beat so hard she could barely hear the surf over the roaring in her ears. 'I regret not making love with you one last time.' She'd ached for just one more memory to hold close to her heart. Even though she knew just one more memory would never have been enough.

The fingers at her waist tightened further, sending spirals of sensation circling through her and making her shift restlessly. He said something low and growly in Italian and then lowered his mouth until his breath caressed her ear. 'I am going to make such love to you, *cara*, you're going to think you've died and gone to heaven.'

Her nipples hardened to instant tight buds and her fingers dug into the hard muscles of his upper arms. 'When?' She didn't care how needy she sounded. She wanted this man and the sooner the better.

'As soon as I can get you alone.'

She closed her eyes on a groan. 'I have to collect Fern from pre-school in an hour.' Fern attended two mornings and one afternoon a week. 'And Benny will wake soon from his nap.'

'*Sì*. It is the way with family life.'

The smile he sent her made her heart expand until it felt too big for her chest. 'I regret not telling you I loved you before I left,' she blurted out.

His entire muscle electrified. 'You love me?'

She nodded, her heart pounding.

He wrapped his arms around her waist and spun her around, his whoop of delight sounding all along the shoreline. And then his mouth was on hers, hot and demanding, and she wrapped her arms around his shoulders as wave after wave of emotion buffeted her.

He lifted his head, long minutes later, his hands

cupping her face, speaking a rush of words in his native tongue.

'What are you saying to me, Luca? My Italian isn't that good.' And every instinct she had told her she wanted to know what he was saying.

Luca smoothed the hair from Monique's face, staring down into the eyes of the woman he loved more than life itself. 'I am telling you that I love you too.'

Her eyes filled with tears and he saw the hope shining there, but then it vanished. 'You don't have to say it back. I'm a big girl, Luca, and—'

'I say it only because it is true. Every person who should have loved and cherished you has let you down—me included—and it has made you maybe afraid to trust again. But I am going to love and cherish you every day and in every way I can think of until you no longer doubt it.'

Her whispered 'Oh!' speared straight to the centre of him.

The water gently caressed their bodies, the swell pushing her against him, tantalising him with her soft lushness. But there was still so much to say. 'I was planning on taking things slowly, not overwhelming you with a declaration of love immediately. I was going to woo you. But you tell me you love me, and I lose control.'

'I like it when you lose control.'

The impish light in her eyes had a groan rising

through him. How could she make him laugh and want, both at the same time?

'I was also telling you how much I want to build a life with you. You, Fern, Benny and I— we are the perfect family. I want you to marry me. Please, say you will marry me?'

Her jaw dropped and every insecurity he'd ever had rushed to the fore. He swore. 'I have made a hash of this.'

Lifting her into his arms, he strode out of the water and onto the beach. Setting her on her feet, he dropped to one knee in the shallow water in front of her. 'Monique, you make my heart sing. Will you do me the honour of making me truly the happiest man in the world and marry me?' He frowned. 'There is a ring back at the house. I didn't bring it because I didn't think it would be—'

She cupped his face. 'The ring doesn't matter.'

Of course it didn't. Not to a woman who delighted in a simple gelato by the Trevi Fountain, preferred to buy her clothes off the rack rather than be clad by famous designers, and who would choose the rustic peace of a Tuscan farmhouse over a Roman *palazzo*. 'I love you, *tesoro mio*. Marry me and I will do everything in my power to make you the happiest woman on earth.'

Confusion clouded her eyes. She leaned down to peer into his face. She was hesitant, this woman. And careful. As she had every right to be. But he would win her trust.

She bit her lip and he realised he'd been staring at it, wondering when he could have another taste. His gaze lowered. The way she leaned towards him gave him a perfect view of the generous curves of her breasts in her swimsuit. His mouth dried and his heart started to thud.

'Oh!' She straightened, pink flushing through her cheeks and down her neck. That's when he noticed her hips were now at eye level and the gently flared curves made his breath catch. He wanted to peel that swimsuit from her body and—

'Stop looking at me like that, Luca!'

'You look good enough to eat, *cara*, and I want to—'

Soft fingers against his mouth shushed him. 'I can't think straight when you look at me like that. And before I answer your question, I need to think.'

He did his best to leash all his baser instincts. He would give her all the time she needed.

'Come on.' She hauled him to his feet. 'We both need to put on a shirt at the very least.'

He swallowed his disappointment that he would not be getting an answer to his question today. *Patience*, he ordered.

Her shirt clung to her wet skin, creating dark patches where her swimsuit was. He pulled his shirt over his head and did what he could to ignore the uncomfortable prickle of his skin contained against cotton when it so hungered to be unfettered.

She spread her towel out and sat at one end, gesturing for him to sit at the other end. He did as she bade, resisting the urge to haul her into his lap so he could nuzzle her neck.

'Luca, I'm so happy you changed your mind about marrying for any other reason than love, but it's still a leap to ask me to marry you.'

She pressed her hands together and he wanted to take them and press them to his lips. 'I love you, Monique. This is why I wish to marry you.'

'But my family is the antithesis of respectable. And I know how hard you've been working to win back the Vieri family's good name. I know how much you want to do that. I know what it means to you.'

He glanced down at his hands for a moment. 'It has taken me a long time to realise that respectability and honour are two very different things.'

He told her then of what his grandfather had done. How he had pressured Anita to remain silent rather than create trouble in Luca's life.

'Your grandfather? But… Oh, Luca, I'm so sorry.' The expression in her eyes told him she knew how betrayed he must feel.

'He didn't plan to keep Benito a secret from me forever. Only until I'd made a suitable marriage.'

'But didn't he know how much it would mean to you? Couldn't he see—?'

She broke off, looking as if she wished she hadn't spoken, and his heart swelled. She didn't want to cause mischief. This woman was only interested in spreading kindness, not spite or trouble.

'Once I learned those facts, I understood that not only did I not want to follow in the path of my parents, but that I did not wish to follow the one my grandfather had trodden either.'

Her eyes never left his face and he ached to kiss her. He resisted the urge. He needed her to know everything.

'I know now that if I want to win my peers' respect and trust, I need to earn it by my actions, by acting with integrity. The only way to re-establish the good name of my family is for all of my generation to show they are people to be respected—to act with honour rather than paying lip service to it and merely giving the appearance of it.'

He lifted her hand to his lips. 'A good man, an honourable man does not let the woman he loves walk away from him without a fight. I let you walk away, and I have never been sorrier for anything in my life. My life has never been so barren.'

She opened her mouth, but he carried on over her. 'There is nothing disreputable in my marrying you, and if anyone thinks otherwise then they are not the kind of people who I either wish to know or want to do business with.'

Her smile, when it came, lit up the entire beach. With a soft cry, she moved towards him and straddled his hips, her hands cupping his face. 'You're going to forge your own path, be your own man.'

'I want to be the best man I can—for my family, for Benny and Fern, but mostly for you, *tesoro*. You make me want to be the best man I can be.'

Her eyes shone. 'You're the best man for me, Luca. That much I do know. And, yes, a thousand times. I would love to marry you.'

And then her arms were around his neck and he was holding her close and nothing had ever felt more perfect in his life.

Eventually, though, she eased back and gave a squeak. 'We have to go and collect Fern!' She shot to her feet, pulling him up with her. 'She's going to be so excited to see you.'

He couldn't wait to see her either.

'And I can't wait to cuddle Benny.' She shook the sand from her towel.

'My family,' he murmured, unable to believe his good fortune.

'Yes, we're a family now, Luca, and the rest of our lives starts right here, right now.' She held her hand out to him. He didn't hesitate. He reached out and took it.

'I'm going to make you all very, *very* happy,' he vowed.

'And we're going to make you very, *very* happy too.'

He gave her a brief blistering kiss. 'I love you, *cara*.'

She smiled back at him with all of that golden caramel warmth that left him in no doubt of her feelings. 'I love you, *il mio cuore*.'

He was her heart, and she was his. And he would cherish her to the end of his days.

* * * * *

*If you enjoyed this story,*
*check out these other great reads from*
*Michelle Douglas*

Billionaire's Road Trip to Forever
Secret Billionaire on Her Doorstep
Singapore Fling with the Millionaire
Redemption of the Maverick Millionaire

*All available now!*